Mills &
Best Seller Romance

A chance to read and collect some of the best-loved novels
from Mills & Boon—the world's largest publisher of
romantic fiction.

Every month, four titles by favourite Mills & Boon authors
will be re-published in the *Best Seller Romance* series.

A list of other titles in the *Best Seller Romance* series
can be found at the end of this book.

Anne Mather

PALE DAWN, DARK SUNSET

MILLS & BOON LIMITED
LONDON · TORONTO

First published in 1975
Australian copyright 1981
Philippine copyright 1981
This edition 1981

© Anne Mather 1975

ISBN 0 263 73634 2

Set in Linocomp Times Roman

*Photoset by Rowland Phototypesetting Limited
Bury St Edmunds, Suffolk.
Made and printed in Great Britain by
Richard Clay (The Chaucer Press) Limited,
Bungay, Suffolk.*

CHAPTER ONE

It was dawn. Already the sky was lightening in the east and a pale apricot gilding was touching the fleecy clouds that shrouded the horizon. Mist rose ghostlike from the trees down in the valley, and the Angelus bell was ringing in the small chapel below. The air was crisp and cool as Rafael came to the door and he breathed deeply, feeling its coldness against the sweating dampness of his flesh.

But it was over, and behind him he could hear the shrill cries the child was still emitting, audible above the relieved protestations of its father. That its mother was alive, too, was due more to the will of God than the skill of its enforced midwives. Franco Maqueras knew nothing about bringing a child into the world, in spite of the fact that this was the seventh daughter his wife had borne him.

But somehow they had succeeded, and Rafael could feel waves of weariness sweeping over his aching body. Only yesterday he had driven a hundred scorching miles to Sustancia to share in the celebration of Mass being held in the new cathedral and then, on his return, Franco had come knocking at his door in the dead of night, begging his help, panic-stricken that his wife was about to bear his child with the overworked doctor many miles away at Pagueri. Rafael had agreed to come, to use the skills which had lain dormant for many months, but in spite of his success he felt no sense of elation, only one of extreme tiredness. His thin cotton shirt and pants were clinging wetly to his skin, and rivulets of sweat, cooling

5

now, mingled with the fine dark hair on his chest. He desired nothing so much as a shower, a change of clothes and a couple of hours' sleep.

But these were luxuries he could not, and would not, have. At least, not for the present. There were more important matters to claim his attention. As he sluiced his face and neck from the pump in the yard he reflected that Father Domenico would be expecting him at the chapel, to join in the early morning Sacrament, and afterwards there was the message from Juan which had been awaiting him on his return last night, requesting his presence at the hacienda. He stretched and wondered with a swiftly suppressed feeling of cynicism whether he had done the right thing in temporarily abandoning his studies in Mexico City to come home to attend his uncle's funeral. His mother had been so appealing, so eager he knew to see her eldest son again after their separation, and he had not refused her. His uncle had worked all his life in the service of the Faith and it was not unreasonable to expect his nephew to attend his burial.

That had been almost two months ago, however, and still he was here in Guadalima. A week, two weeks at the most, he had expected to be away from the seminary, but circumstances had served to detain him. Father Domenico was beginning to rely on his assistance, the people of the villages brought their problems to him, he was becoming involved again . . .

He thrust long lean fingers through the thick strength of his hair. Soon, he told himself urgently, soon he must return to the seminary, to finish his studies, to accept whatever responsibilities would be placed upon him once he became a member of the priesthood. His life would not be here in this remote, fertile valley in the highlands of the Chiapas where his family had lived for generations, but possibly thousands of miles away in some other part of the vast American continent.

He turned back to enter the one-roomed dwelling where the Maqueras and their five surviving children lived and ate and slept, and encountered Franco Maqueras just behind him. The Mexican's broad features creased into a smile and he spread his thick peasant's hands extravagantly.

"What can I say, *señor*?" he demanded. "I am most grateful for all you have done. Without you . . . " He made an expressive gesture. "I am in your debt, *señor*."

Rafael shook his head. "No, my friend, not my debt. You must thank God for your wife's deliverance. I did nothing more than serve as his instrument."

"Oh, but yes, *señor,* of course, *señor*!" Franco crossed himself piously. "But you understand I am so relieved that Maria is well and that the child is healthy that I do not always make myself clear. If there is anything I can do, any service I can perform for you—"

"I know, I know." Rafael flexed his aching back muscles and went past him into the room, reaching for the cotton denim jacket he had shed the night before. Maria Maqueras was lying prostrate among the tumbled covers, the baby a squirming bundle in the shawl beside her. A flicker of impatience momentarily darkened his features and then he gave a characteristic shrug of his shoulders. It was not for him to question the burden this extra mouth to feed would place on the family. These people were taught to accept their lot and be thankful. Only occasionally he experienced doubts that life should be built on so precarious a premise, but these he determinedly squashed.

"You'll call Doctor Rodrigues as soon as he gets back?" he confirmed with Franco, and the other man nodded vigorously.

"But of course, *señor*. No doubt he will be glad it is over without needing his assistance." He moved his head philosophically from side to side.

Rafael nodded, hesitating a moment as he saw the

greyness in Maria's face. The woman was exhausted. But in a few short days she would be required to take up her duties as wife and mother to her husband and the six children with whom he had now provided her. How would she cope? How could she be expected to wash and clean and prepare food with the baby draining every last ounce of strength from her scrawny breasts? His hands curled into fists. This was not his concern. He could feel sympathy—compassion; but that was all. He could offer no alternative.

After a final word with Franco he crossed the yard where skinny chickens scratched a living and climbed into the dust-smeared Landrover that belonged to the estate. He raised a hand in farewell and started the engine with a flick of his wrist. He drove away from the humble collection of dwellings that clung to the mountainside down a track from which dust spurted liberally, creating a cloud of mud behind him.

The sun was rising and below him he could see the fertile acres of the valley thick with wheat and fruit orchards, exotic with colour and brilliance. This valley had been his home for more than thirty years, it was his heritage, the Cueras estate which his brother Juan now ran had been his inheritance.

But he had not wanted it. From an early age, he had been more interested in feeding the mind than the body, and the people and their problems had always been his primary concern. He and his father had clashed on that. The estate had been in the family's hands for more than three hundred years, since the days of the *conquistadores*. His ancestor, Alberto Cueras, had been a rich and influential man in the old country—in Spain—but when he had come upon this fertile valley he had abandoned his ideas of returning to his homeland. He had built a house and put down roots, sent for his wife and children; and in the years that followed expanded his holding until today it was the largest in the district. Eldest son had followed eldest son, always working for the estate, always making more money, exploiting the workers and using the women for their own pleasure. Of course, in recent years, things had changed a little; large estates were no longer so common, although in these remote districts the quality of life had changed little over the centuries.

But Rafael had rebelled. Taught from childhood to take whatever he wanted as his right, he had followed his father's example until its very selfishness had sickened him. He had been appalled the first time he had discovered his father had mistresses, but under his father's guidance he had become accustomed to winning the affections of any woman that took his fancy. In truth, he had encountered no opposition. His lean frame and dark good looks had disarmed the most reluctant *doncellas* and he was always generous to those he pursued.

And then he went to university, and away from his father's influence his innate decency began to assert itself. He no longer found the satisfaction of the senses an adequate substitute for books and learning and his studies began to occupy more and more of his time. During his vacations, the poverty of the *peons* or peasant workers, the deplorable housing conditions, the spread of disease—these things began to trouble him, and he no longer felt any identification with the inanimate chunk of land that was his heritage.

He didn't really know what he would have done had his father still been alive. He knew the decision to abdicate from his responsibilities to the estate would have appalled him. But his father had died from a heart attack while Rafael was taking his degree in medicine, and it had been natural that his younger brother, Juan, who had never shown any intellectual leanings, and who had been there at the hacienda at the time of his father's death, should take over the running of the estate in Rafael's absence.

After that, for a while at least, he had been content.

9

He was able to practise medicine and things had been good. But restlessness had followed hard on the heels of his mother's increasingly frequent urgings that it was time he got married, fathered sons to ensure the continuation of the Cueras line. Rafael had had no desire to get married, to have children. His youthful decadence had left its mark on him, and the placid Spanish girls produced for his delectation aroused no sexual interest in him. On the contrary, he had serious doubts that any woman could attract him now. And besides, he wanted to serve the community, not his family. And so, in spite of his mother's tears and recriminations, he had taken the short step from uncertainty to the seminary . . .

Now the Landrover was crossing the plain scythed by the rushing, gleaming waters of the Rio Lima. On either side of the river stretched acres of wheat and maize fields. Lush vegetation sprang up the wooded walls of the valley, interspersed here and there by the brown thatched roofs of peasant dwellings.

Far across the valley, on a rise in the lower slopes he could see the rambling walls of a larger, more imposing building. This was the Hacienda Cueras, the place where he had been born, where he had lived until he went to university, where his mother and brother and younger sisters lived. But their demand of his services would have to wait for the present.

He crossed the river by means of a wooden bridge, its patched slats bearing witness to the numerous occasions it had been partially swept away by the rain-swollen waters. He could hear the chapel bells, too, increasing in persistence. Just ahead of him now, set among trees, the Capilla de los Inocentes looked like a bride dressed for her wedding. Its grey walls were hung with purple and white blossoms, tiny star-shaped flowers in the colours of the Eucharist. Already he could see women hurrying up the worn stone steps, drawing black scarves over their heads, and he felt the familiar sense of well-being that always came from this duty. This was what he wanted, he told himself. Everything else came after.

Later in the morning, when the sun was climbing steadily to its zenith, Rafael drove through the wide stone gateway that gave access to the grounds of the hacienda. Although it was still early the shutters were thrown wide, and the scent of beeswax which he always associated with its polished floors was in the air. He could remember sliding across them as a child, incurring the wrath of Jezebel, the housekeeper, who always knew who to blame when she found skidding marks of muddy feet marring the shiny surface. Jezebel, Rafael smiled. Whoever had chosen her name had paid little heed to the connotations of her namesake.

He walked into the wide hall and looked about him appreciatively. It was a beautiful old building and it never failed to please him. This hall, the two rooms adjoining, and the gallery above were all that was left of the original building, but successive generations had added to its bulk, strengthening its foundations and rebuilding where necessary so that today it rambled over half an acre, split level, and partially two-storied. The furnishings, much of them antique, had the worn patina of years upon them, but its faded elegance went well with the heavily carved panelling and baroque iron-work.

"Senor Rafael!"

The housekeeper's voice was filled with warmth and devotion. So far as Jezebel was concerned, Rafael was still master here. She came towards him eagerly from the door at the back of the hall which led to the kitchens and servants' quarters, taking one of his hands in both of hers.

"Good morning, Jezebel." Rafael looked kindly on the elderly Indian woman who had served his family for over thirty years and who still ran the household with a rod of iron. "I had a message that Juan wanted to see me. Do you know where he is?"

Jezebel released his hand with reluctance, her fingers indicating the lines of sleeplessness around his eyes. "You do not take care of yourself in that little hut down in the village," she exclaimed.

Rafael was patient. "It's hardly a hut, Jezebel," he protested mildly. "Where is my brother?"

'Señor Juan is breakfasting on the patio, *señor*. You have had breakfast?"

"As a matter of fact, no." Rafael shook his head.

Jezebel glared at him disapprovingly. "You see? You do not eat—you do not sleep—"

"Jezebel, I had work to do last night—"

"Ay, ay!" Jezebel nodded her head. "Of course. I am remembering. It was the Maqueras woman, was it not? Her time had come. Her husband—he come here looking for you last night—very late!"

"That's right." Rafael moved his shoulders wearily. "Maria had another daughter. And now—I must see Juan."

"I will bring you coffee and *croissants, señor*," insisted Jezebel firmly, and Rafael inclined his head.

"That would be very nice, Jezebel," he agreed, and with a faint smile he passed her and walked through the arched entrance to the reception lounge which opened out onto the patio at the back of the house.

Juan Cueras was seated in a cane-latticed chair at the glass topped table. He was like Rafael, yet unlike. Rafael was tall, lean and dark, his features clearly defined. Juan was not so tall and thicker set, and yet the similarity was there in the darkness of their skin, the curve of their brows, the thin firmness of their mouths. Juan's mouth was perhaps a little fuller, a little more sensual, but that was only to be expected in a man who did not share his brother's desire for asceticism. He looked up now, as Rafael came through the long glass doors to join him, thickly spreading an apricot preserve over the *croissant* in his hand. He took a mouthful, nodding at his brother in welcome, and then wiping his lips with a napkin he said:

"Good morning, Rafael. I see you got my message."

"Did you doubt it?" Rafael lounged into the chair opposite his brother, flicking an insect from his sleeve. "But I'd be obliged if you'd be brief. I have a lot to get through today."

Juan finished the *croissant* with evident relish, and poured himself more coffee, offering the jug to Rafael.

"Jezebel's bringing me some more," said Rafael, shaking his head. "She has this inescapable idea that I'm not looking after myself."

"You're not." Juan was candid. "I simply can't understand—" He broke off. "But we've had that argument before." He pushed a jug of freshly squeezed orange juice towards the other man. "Go ahead—have some. I don't enjoy eating alone."

Rafael took the glass that was proffered and poured himself some of the fresh fruit juice. He tasted it experimentally and then, finding it to his taste, drained the glass.

"That's better," remarked Juan with a smile. "Don't you think you deny yourself enough without including food?"

"I eat enough," replied Rafael quietly, toying with the empty glass. "It's perhaps a question of how little one needs. One should not gorge oneself when half the population of the world is dying of starvation."

"And do you think if I deprived myself of one more *croissant*—one extra cup of coffee, I would be doing anything to aid those starving peoples?" exclaimed Juan impatiently

"We have had this argument before, Juan, as you pointed out," observed Rafael, pushing the glass away from him.

13

Jezebel appeared with a laden tray, setting it down on the table and setting out a second coffee pot, cream and sugar, *croissants* and curls of butter, and more of the thick apricot conserve.

"Now you make a good meal, *señor*," she instructed severely, casting a less than respectful glance in Juan's direction. "Your brother, for once, can show you a good example!"

Rafael hid a smile as he obediently lifted a *croissant* on to his plate and spread it thinly with butter. Jezebel waited a moment to satisfy herself that he did indeed intend to eat it and then went away, muttering imprecations against anyone who neglected the common necessities of life.

Juan waited until Rafael was tackling his second *croissant* and then he said: "I wish you to do something for me, Rafael."

Rafael looked up. "Yes?"

"Yes." Juan felt about his person for his case of cheroots. "You remember the child from the mission, do you not?"

Rafael frowned. "The English girl—of course."

Juan nodded, putting a cheroot between his teeth and making a second search for his lighter. "Yes. Well, it appears that her name may be Lucy Carmichael."

"May be?"

"That is correct. As the child has apparently forgotten who she is, it is impossible to say with any certainty who she might be. But aboard this aircraft which crashed several weeks ago there was a family called Carmichael; mother, father—and daughter of some eight years."

"I see. And you think this might be the child found by Benito Santos?"

"Well, it may be."

"But is that possible? Where did this aircraft crash?"

"In the mountains—some eighteen miles from here."

Rafael wiped his mouth with the back of his hand. "It

14

seems a remote possibility."

"But a possibility nevertheless. And unfortunately the authorities have insisted that I investigate every possibility."

"Unfortunately?" Rafael was intrigued.

"Yes, unfortunately. You must know that the child has taken a liking to me—that I have had her here several times to visit."

Rafael lay back in his chair viewing Juan through narrowed eyes and his brother felt a fleeting sense of envy that Rafael could exude such an aura of latent sensuality without any apparent effort. It was not fair in someone who was prepared to deny even his own masculinity. "But what were your intentions towards the child?" he asked curiously.

Juan sighed. "I don't know. It's too soon to say. I may have considered adoption—"

"Adoption?" Rafael lifted his shoulders in surprise. "But she may have relatives."

"She has." Juan got irritably to his feet. "That is why I need your assistance."

"My assistance?" Rafael shook his head. "I'm sorry, I seem to repeat everything you say. But I do not see what I can do."

Juan puffed impatiently at his cheroot. "If you wait a moment, I will explain." He walked round his brother's chair and back to the table again. "The authorities have discovered that there is someone—an aunt—the sister of the child's mother." He drew a deep breath. "As one would expect, she lives in England."

"And has she been informed of the possibility that her niece may still be alive?"

Juan nodded. "Yes. Yes, she has. And that is how you can help me."

Rafael frowned. "Yes?"

"Yes." Juan licked his lips. "This woman is on her way to Guadalima to see the child—to find out for herself whether indeed she is this Lucy Carmichael."

"I see." Rafael inclined his head. "But how can I be of assistance?"

"Wait—wait!" Juan was obviously finding it difficult to put into actual words what he wanted his brother to do. He drew deeply on his cheroot and seated himself opposite Rafael again, resting his elbows rather nervously on the table. "You see, Rafael, it is like this. This woman—her name is Lord, *Miss* Lord—is arriving from England tomorrow. I—well, I want you to meet her!"

"Me?" Rafael was taken aback. "Why me? Where is she arriving?"

"Mexico City, where else?"

"Juan!" Rafael stared at his brother incredulously. "You cannot be serious! I cannot go to Mexico City to meet this woman. She does not know me. I hardly know the child. If you wish to see her you must meet her yourself."

Juan flung himself back in his seat. He heaved a heavy sigh and spread his hands expressively. "You ask me this?" He shook his head. "What am I to say to her?"

"What am *I* to say to her?" remarked Rafael dryly.

"It is different for you," exclaimed Juan, leaning towards his brother again. "You are used to talking to people—you have—authority. And besides, you have a much better grasp of the English language than I have."

Rafael poured himself some coffee. "And this is why you sent for me?"

"Yes."

Rafael drank some of the black coffee reflectively. "I do not understand all of this," he said at last. "Why are the authorities not arranging for this woman to be brought to Guadalima?"

"Father Esteban at the mission left the matter in my hands."

"I see. And what do you hope to achieve?"

Juan coloured slightly. "Achieve? That is a curious

word to use, Rafael. It smacks of conspiracy."

Rafael shook his head. "On the contrary, what you wish to do for this child is admirable. I just cannot think that Valentina will welcome a ready-made daughter into your household."

"Valentina and I are not married yet, Rafael."

"No." Rafael conceded that point slowly. "Even so, you know that it is expected."

Juan scowled. "Will you meet the woman? *Madre de Dios*, Rafael, what would I find to say to some middle-aged spinster? How could I explain my feelings for the child? If she is this Lucy Carmichael, how can I persuade her that the child might be happier here with us than taken back to that cold and unfeeling country of her birth?"

Rafael half smiled. "I think you are being rather uncharitable, Juan," he commented mildly. "You really know nothing about England, and the child may be content to return with her aunt—a blood relation. After all, seeing her aunt again may restore her memory."

"I know, I know. Do you think I have not thought of that?" Juan sounded impatient. "That is why I wish you to speak with this woman—this Miss Lord. I want you to tell her about me—to explain that I am not a villain with designs on her niece. I want you to explain that the child herself likes me, that I find her enchanting. And that for her aunt to take her away without first considering what she might be depriving her of would be—how shall I say?—precipitate?"

"In other words, you want me to extol your praises," observed Rafael ironically. "You think perhaps she might then look more kindly on the possibilities of leaving the child here?"

Juan tapped his nails irritably against the glass surface of the table. Across the patio a walled rose garden was giving off a fragrant perfume, and humming birds vied with the butterflies for brilliance. He turned back to his

17

brother. "And you, Rafael? Do you not think the child would be happier here, amongst all this?" He spread his hands again. "This woman—this aunt—she cannot possibly give her what I can give her."

"How do you know that?"

Juan sighed. "It is obvious. The child's clothes—the pitiful things she was found in were not the garments of a rich child. Her reactions to everything I have done for her have not been the reactions of a child already satiated by luxury."

"And might she not have forgotten these things also?"

"No. Ordinary every day things, she remembers. It is the personal details she has forgotten," Juan pressed out the stub of his cheroot in the onyx ashtray. "The doctors are confident that she will recover. It is only a matter of time. I have had Delgado out from Mexico City—"

"Ramon Delgado?"

"Yes. Do you know him?"

"As a matter of fact we were at university together."

"I see." Juan's lips twisted. "Well, as I say, Delgado expresses the opinion that it is only a matter of time before her memory returns completely. Needless to say, this news arouses mixed feelings inside me. Naturally I want her to regain her faculties, but I am afraid if this woman comes here—stimulates the child's recollective abilities and then takes her away without first giving her a chance to decide for herself—"

"But you say the child is only some eight years old?"

"That's right."

"Then how can she decide what would be best for her future? Juan, you have to accept that in this instance you are helpless."

"No, I will not accept that." Juan's face was grim. He turned again to his brother. "Rafael, I ask very little of you—surely it is not too much to ask you to help me in this . . ."

18

Rafael sighed now. "I don't see how anything I can say can make the slightest difference."

Juan hesitated. Then he said: "Rafael, you have influence. Won't you use it? The influence of your position?"

Rafael had known this was coming, of course. "Juan," he said patiently, "Juan, I have no influence, I am nothing yet."

"But you will be soon. You already assist Father Domenico—"

"In a lay capacity only!" Rafael shook his head and pushed aside his dirty cup and plate. "These people, Juan—the Carmichaels—were they Catholics?"

Juan moved his shoulders awkwardly. "I—no! I believe they belonged to the Church of England."

Rafael's hand descended heavily on the table. "And you expect this woman to leave her niece—the only surviving member of her sister's family—with you, the brother of a man who may ultimately become a priest in the Roman Catholic Church?"

Juan's jaw moved spasmodically. "So you won't help me?"

"I don't see how I can."

"Then you're not listening to me, Rafael. What can this woman—this aunt—give the girl? She is not even married! She does not have the support of a husband. She is a secretary or something with some firm in London. She has no money—no influence—no position in society!"

"These things are not so important to some people," pointed out Rafael quickly. "And I do not speak only for myself. If this woman lives alone, she may be glad of the child's companionship."

"But how can she care for her? If she is at work all day, how will she manage? Always supposing she can *afford* to support her."

"If you really want to help the child then perhaps you ought to offer to support her in the manner in which you

19

would like to see her."

Juan stared at Rafael in astonishment. "No! No, I could not do that."

Rafael shrugged. "It was a suggestion, nothing more."

Juan looked thoughtful. "Will you not do as I ask and meet this woman at least.?" he appealed. He paused. "It may just be—possible to persuade her to change her mind . . ."

Rafael's face darkened. "Juan! You would not—offer her money?"

Juan moved uncomfortably. "Did I say I might?"

"It was implicit in your words." Rafael's jaw hardened and he thrust back his chair and got abruptly to his feet. "Very well, I will meet your Miss Lord. But only because I am afraid that if I refuse you will think of some other way to keep the child." He shook his head. "I have never known you to be so obsessed with another human being."

Juan could smile now that he had got what he wanted. "I would not call it an obsession, Rafael. I am fond of the child, I admit it. It pleasures me that she treats me like the father she has lost. It is a—satisfying sensation to feel oneself the centre of a child's world."

"And when she recovers her memory? What then? The realisation of the loss of her parents must eventually be faced."

"I know it. But I am hoping that by then the life I have given her here will compensate—"

"And if it does not?"

Juan's lips tightened. "We will face that contingency if and when it occurs." Then: "Now, you will go and see our mother, will you not? You know she would be heartbroken if she learned you had visited the hacienda without spending some time with her."

Rafael nodded, thrusting his hands deeply into his trousers pockets. He would have preferred to leave the

20

hacienda forthwith, to go back to his own house and ponder the disquieting aspects of the situation while he bathed and changed his clothes. But it was not to be. He sighed. He had not realised when he left Mexico City how much more difficult it was to remain detached from the intimacies of one's own family. The seminary had been a refuge from the everyday problems of living, and he admitted he had enjoyed its isolation. But here, involved as he was, he could feel emotions stirring inside him that had been long suppressed. He must not make judgments, he told himself impatiently. He was the outsider here, it was not really his affair. But his intelligence told him that this was just a whim on Juan's part which could easily be replaced by another.

His mother was still in bed when he entered her room at the head of the stairs. It was a beautiful room, the floor coolly mosaiced, and strewn with rugs in cinnamon and gold. Wide windows opened on to a balcony, edged with wrought iron, which overhung the patio, and a cool breeze stirred the lemon chiffon draperies. The bed, a magnificent fourposter which was said to date back to the eighteenth century, was wide and comfortable, and Rafael's mother was ensconced among the soft pillows. A used breakfast tray was pushed to one side and she was reading a newspaper until, at the advent of her son, she thrust it swiftly aside and held out both hands to him.

Rafael greeted her warmly, taking her hands in his and bending to kiss her perfumed cheek. Then he released himself and took up a stance before the open balcony doors.

"So you are going to Mexico City to meet this woman, Rafael," remarked Doña Isabella softly.

Rafael glanced significantly behind him. "You heard?"

"It would have been impossible to do otherwise. Juan is so vehement." His mother sighed, plucking at the silk

21

coverlet. "You do not think he should do this."

Rafael shrugged. "I am only afraid . . ." He shook his head. "Juan is old enough to make his own decisions."

Doña Isabella shook her head. "Is he? I wonder?" She stared penetratingly at her eldest son, a troubled expression marring her smooth olive features. "Rafael—Rafael, if you do go to Mexico City, you will come back, won't you?"

Rafael's face relaxed. "Of course. How else is this woman to find her way here? But soon—soon I must return to the seminary."

His mother pressed her lips together. "Not too soon, Rafael, not too soon."

"I've been here two months already," he protested.

"I know, I know. But we see so little of you, my darling. You so rarely come to the hacienda . . ."

Rafael made an apologetic gesture. "There is so much for me to do—" he was beginning, when his mother interrupted him bitterly.

"I know. Everyone demands your time, your advice, your medical knowledge, while I—your mother—am spared only a few minutes every week!"

Rafael approached the bed helplessly, sitting down beside her and taking her hands in his again. "*Madre mia*, I am sorry," he muttered huskily, guilt at his neglect of her overwhelming him. He raised her fingers to his lips and kissed them gently. "But you must understand that I cannot deny Rodrigues my help."

Doña Isabella laid a hand on his dark head, smoothing the unruly vitality of his hair. Then she sighed. "I am sorry, too, Rafael. I am a selfish old woman. But knowing you are in the valley and not living here at the hacienda . . . Could you not come and stay with us?"

Rafael released her hands and spread his own expressively. "You know that the hacienda is too far from the village. The house I have is easily accessible, and besides, I can be alone there."

"And this is important to you, isn't it?" His mother's voice had a note of acceptance in it now. "Very well, Rafael, I won't insist that you come and stay here. But surely—after this trip to Mexico City—you could spend a little more time with us? After all, when you leave the valley, Rodrigues will have to manage, will he not?"

Rafael got to his feet. "Very well, *Madrecita*. I will come as often as I can. But now—" He glanced at the plain gold watch on his wrist, "now I must go. I am hot and dirty and I need a shower. Besides, I must tell Father Domenico that I shall be leaving for Mexico City first thing in the morning."

"You will take the helicopter to Puebla?"

Rafael nodded. "Yes. I presume there is a car there I can use."

"A Mustang." His mother inclined her head. "As I recall it, Juan bought two." She bit her lip. "But you will drive carefully, won't you, Rafael? The roads can be so dangerous."

Rafael smiled, revealing his even white teeth. "You worry too much, *Madrecita*." He kissed her once more and then moved towards the door. "I will see you tomorrow evening. When I deliver Miss Lord."

"Very well, Rafael. Take care!"

Rafael bade her goodbye and went down the stairs slowly. Now that he was free to go he was curiously loath to do so. This house had been his home for so many years and he knew a fleeting temptation to go to his old room and use the bathroom there. He knew his room remained as it was when he had left it. His mother insisted on it always being ready and available to him. But such temptations were never overwhelming and he walked across the wide hall and out onto the steps above the forecourt.

Two girls were dismounting from their horses in the shadow of the Landrover, assisted by a dark-skinned Mexican stableboy, and Rafael recognised his two

23

younger sisters, Carla and Constancia. They were eighteen-year-old twins, the last children his father had sired before his fatal illness. When they saw Rafael they came exuberantly towards him, hugging him enthusiastically and protesting that he could not leave yet.

"I must," insisted Rafael, disentangling himself from their clinging hands. "I have things to do."

"I expect Juan has been asking you to go and meet this woman—this aunt of the little one's—for him, hasn't he?" suggested Carla perceptively. "Are you going?"

Rafael's expression was wry. "As a matter of fact, I am."

"I don't think you should." That was Constancia, the quieter, more introspective of the two. "Let Juan meet her himself!"

"I agree," chimed in Carla. "Why should you have to waste your time going to meet some stuffy old maid?"

"That will do, Carla." Rafael's mouth turned down at the corners. "You know absolutely nothing about Miss Lord, and I do not think we should make wild statements about someone who is totally anonymous to us."

Carla pouted. "Can I come with you?"

Rafael shook his head. "I don't think that would be a very good idea."

"Why not? At least you wouldn't be bored—"

"I am never bored, Carla," returned Rafael grimly, and climbed determinedly into the Landrover. "I'll see you both tomorrow evening. When I get back."

Constancia came to the door of the vehicle and touched his arm. "I wish I could come with you, Rafael," she murmured wistfully, and for a moment he was tempted. But then he caught sight of Carla's indignant face and realised he could not possibly take one without the other.

"There wouldn't be room in the helicopter," he replied, touching her cheek with a lean finger. "I'll see you tomorrow, hmm?"

24

Constancia stepped back reluctantly and Rafael put the Landrover into gear. Then he drove swiftly down the drive and out on to the track to the village.

CHAPTER TWO

THE international airport at Mexico City was a seething mass of humanity in the heat of the late afternoon. More and more people were discovering the fascination for the past which gave the Aztec civilisation such an irresistible appeal. Where once only scientists and historians came to investigate the relics of that ancient culture there now thronged safari-shirted tourists, slung about with cameras and binoculars, and all the other paraphernalia of the cult fanatic.

Rafael disliked the crowds. He avoided them whenever possible. And the reasons for his being here at all were gradually arousing an unmistakable feeling of irritation inside him. The aircraft bringing this woman who might or might not be the child's aunt out from England had developed an engine fault and had been delayed twenty-four hours in Kingston, which had meant that Rafael had had to book in at the airport hotel and spend a whole day kicking his heels. But finally the flight's arrival had been announced, and he walked reluctantly towards the reception area. His hands were thrust deep into the pockets of his close-fitting corduroy pants and as he wore no jacket because it was so hot, his thin cream knitted shirt clung to his skin. He was hardly aware that several pairs of female eyes turned speculatively in his direction. He was simply not interested. He was totally absorbed with the disruptive quality of his own thoughts.

The plane had landed by the time he reached reception, and because of the delay in Jamaica and certain formalities which had been conducted there the passengers were quickly dealt with. Luggage was unloaded and gradually the passengers trickled through to collect their belongings and be greeted by welcoming relatives and friends.

Rafael stood to one side, his feet slightly apart, assessing all the women who emerged with equal penetration. There were several middle-aged women and his stomach muscles tautened when he contemplated approaching one of them with his brother's proposition. But fortunately they were all quickly encompassed into welcoming groups and Rafael viewed the men that followed without interest. Most of the passengers looked relieved that the journey was over and he conceded that knowing one's aircraft had developed an engine fault on the first leg of the journey could not make for a comfortable completion.

A woman in a wheelchair came next, propelled by a tall girl who looked round the reception area with curious eyes. Rafael frowned. Could this perhaps be Miss Lord? This woman in the wheelchair who looked rather pale and drawn.

But no! He stifled his increasing impatience as a man and a woman approached them and bent to speak consolingly to the woman in the chair. Then they spoke to the girl and she smiled, and said something which from her manner appeared to be deprecating their obvious gratitude.

Rafael looked away. Where was the woman? he silently demanded, feeling his reserves of tolerance running desperately low. Surely she would have the sense to realise that someone would be sent to meet her! Surely she wouldn't leave the confines of the airport and seek accommodation at some hotel?

"Excuse me, *señor!*"

The feminine voice to one side of him broke into his absorption and his brows drew together in a scowl as he

27

turned to look at the girl who had spoken. She was the girl who had been propelling the wheelchair and at once his spirits rose a little. Could it be that the woman in the wheelchair was Miss Lord, after all?

"*Si?*" He was abrupt, but he couldn't help it.

The girl smiled, seemingly unconcerned by his uncompromising attitude. Objectively, he had to concede that she was an unusually attractive young woman. She was tall, perhaps five feet six or seven, and without the angular thinness sometimes associated with girls of her height. She was slim, but not excessively so, and firm breasts were moulded beneath the thin cotton of her shirt. A mass of straight red-gold hair fell in a heavy curtain about her shoulders, her features were even, her eyes an amazing shade of green and fringed by dark, gold-tipped lashes, her mouth full and mobile. She was dressed in the kind of casual attire affected by the youth of the day—cotton denim jeans that clung to her hips and tapered at the ankle, thonged sandals on her bare feet. A canvas holdall was draped over her shoulder drawing attention to the open neck of her shirt where the smooth column of her throat was clearly visible. Without a doubt, he decided, she was not unaccustomed to the ready admiration of the opposite sex. It was there in the slightly slanting eyes, in her awareness, in the confidence she exuded—and Rafael withdrew behind a façade of coldness that was totally alien to him.

"Excuse me," she said again, and her voice was warm and husky and unmistakably English. "But you're not by any chance—Señor Cueras?"

Rafael stiffened. "I am Rafael Cueras," he agreed politely.

"Oh, I see. *Rafael!*" The girl looked disappointed. "I'm sorry. It was a Señor Juan Cueras I was looking for."

Rafael drew himself up to his full height and looked down at her. "Juan Cueras is my brother, *señorita*. Do you speak to me on behalf of Miss Lord?"

"On behalf of,—" The girl broke off. "Oh, no, *señor*. I don't speak on behalf of anybody. I *am* Miranda Lord!"

To say Rafael was surprised would be a masterpiece of understatement. He was astounded, flabbergasted! He stared at the girl as though she had just announced her intention to stick a knife in his ribs. He couldn't believe it, he couldn't. That this female—this girl—was the expected aunt from England! It wasn't possible. Aunts in his country were middle-aged to elderly women attired in black, not slips of creatures little more than children themselves.

Miranda Lord was smiling at his amazement. "Is something wrong?" she enquired in an amused voice. "Am I not what you were expecting?"

That she should so precisely put her finger on what was wrong irritated him. He disliked the way she was looking at him, the way her eyes mocked his confusion. "I—no, *señorita,*" he retorted curtly. "You are perhaps—younger, that is all."

She nodded. "Well, my sister was twelve years older," she conceded, a cloud of remembered grief darkening her eyes for a moment. Then she shook her head impatiently. "I'm sorry if I'm a disappointment to you."

The amusement was back again and Rafael cast a swift look around them. He realised they could not go on standing here when at any moment another aircraft would be landing and other passengers would be crowding this lounge, but he was curiously loath to take responsibility for her. Still, it had to be done.

"You will please to come with me, *señorita,*" he directed, his English worsening as his irritation irrationally increased. "You have suitcases?"

Miranda looked across the room. "Only one. That's it over there. I'll get it."

"I will get it, *señorita.*"

29

Rafael strode away and picked up the square black case, noting its battered edges with a tightening of his lips. It was obvious that the situation was as Juan had suggested. This girl had no money, and was certainly not the kind of guardian he would have chosen for a child of eight years. For the first time he felt a small sympathy towards his brother's cause. Perhaps Juan was right after all.

He came back to the girl, and she said: "You don't have to keep calling me *señorita*. My name is Miranda. I'm used to that."

Rafael made no reply to this but merely indicated that she should accompany him across the well-lit entrance hall and out into the cooling warmth of the late afternoon.

"I expect you've been waiting since yesterday, haven't you?" Miranda suggested, as they walked to where Rafael had left the car. "I'm sorry. The plane developed a fault. It was quite nerve-racking really."

But she didn't appear to be suffering any ill-effects, thought Rafael with unusual cynicism, and despised himself for feeling that way.

"Aren't those flowers beautiful!" she was exclaiming now, spreading her hands and giving a little shake of her shoulders. "I can hardly believe it, you know. That I'm here—in Mexico. I've done very little travelling, I'm afraid."

Rafael's nostrils flared. "I should have thought that the reasons behind this journey were less than stimulating, *señorita*."

She glanced sideways at him, and her eyes were coolly appraising. Tall as he was, she did not have to look up far into his face and it was rather disconcerting to him. Most of the people he associated with, men as well as his mother and sisters, were much smaller than he was.

Now she said quietly: "My sister and her husband went missing more than four months ago. I've had to

30

adjust myself to the fact that they're never coming back."

Rafael felt reproved and didn't care for the experience. He was guiltily aware that he was making a very poor impression, but he said nothing and she looked away again, making some further comment about the banks of blossom that fronted the airport buildings.

The grey Mustang gleamed metal-like on the stark concrete apron of the parking area. Miranda silently admired its sleek elegance and then asked: "Yours?"

Rafael shook his head. "My brother's, *señorita*." He swung open the passenger door. "Won't you please get in?"

With a shrug she curved herself into the seat and he stowed her case in the boot before joining her. It was some time since he had driven any woman other than a member of his own family, and he could smell the faint aroma of some perfume she was wearing and feel the warmth from her skin close beside his.

They swung out of the parking area and he was relieved to have the traffic to rivet his attention. He was conscious of her looking about her with interest and in an effort to behave naturally he pointed out the twin mountain peaks which have become world-famous since the Spanish conqueror Cortes viewed the Aztec city from the tableland between them. They did not drive into Mexico City, however, but swung away south towards Puebla. If she was disappointed that she was not to have some time in the capital Rafael couldn't help it. If she wished to go sightseeing when the business which had brought her to Mexico was over, that was her affair.

All the same, he realised belatedly he had not offered her a meal before embarking on this journey, and sooner or later he would have to bring up the question of the child. He was not looking forward to that.

"How far is it to Guadalima?" she asked suddenly, as

31

clouds began to obscure the slanting rays of the setting sun.

"Some distance yet, *señorita*." Rafael paused. "I did not think of it at the airport, but perhaps you are hungry?"

Miranda shook her head. "Not particularly. We had a meal on the plane." She looked down at her nails. "Tell me—I understood your brother was to meet me—is—is he ill or something?"

Rafael's fingers tightened on the wheel. "No. No, not ill, *señorita*."

"But there must have been some reason, mustn't there?" she insisted, her eyes challenging his. "After all, you didn't want to come, did you?"

Rafael was taken aback. "Why do you say that."

"It's obvious." She slid lower into her seat, drawing up her foot and draping her arms round her knee. "I get the feeling I'm something more than a nuisance."

Rafael was contrite. "I'm sorry," he said stiffly.

She wrinkled her nose. "No, you're not. I'm just trying to work out why you should come to meet me if you feel this way."

Rafael sighed and a little of the tension went out of him. "You must forgive me, *señorita*. I am a little—tired."

She shook her head. "Tell me about Lucy."

Rafael hesitated. "You're sure the child is Lucy, then?"

"Well, I've seen a photograph of her, sent by this priest, Father—Estoban?" He nodded and she went on: "It's not the best photograph I've seen of her, but it certainly looks like her. And I don't suppose there are too many children wandering about Mexico answering her description."

"No." Rafael had to admit that.

"I understand your—brother—has been very good to her."

32

This was his opportunity, but Rafael did not immediately take it. He had the feeling that this girl was different from any contingency Juan had considered. And he wasn't altogether sure that she would be prepared to abandon her niece however tempting the offer.

Now he said: "My brother has grown very attached to—to the child."

She nodded. "So I understand from the priest. I must thank him for taking such an interest in her. Does your brother have no children of his own?"

"My brother is not yet married, *señorita*," replied Rafael dryly, but she merely smiled.

"I see." Her eyes danced. "Then of course he couldn't have, could he?" But he sensed she was laughing at him again.

Rafael's lips thinned. "As a matter of fact Juan is—betrothed, *señorita*."

"Oh!" She drew her lower lip between her teeth. "And you, *señor*? Are you married? Do you have children?"

"No!" Rafael shook his head.

She raised dark eyebrows. "You sound very definite about that." She shrugged. "Nor am I. But I always imagined people married younger in Latin countries."

"Not everyone wishes to get married, *señorita*," he was stung to retort.

"No. No, I realise that. It's going out of fashion, isn't it?"

"That was not what I meant, *señorita*."

"Wasn't it?" Her eyes flickered over the open neck of his shirt, lingering for a while on the hair-roughened skin of his chest before continuing down to his bare forearms where he had rolled back his sleeves. She contemplated the plain gold watch on his wrist and then dropped her eyes to her hands.

No woman of his own race that Rafael had ever known had looked at him in quite that way before, and he felt annoyed. Had she no respect, this girl from England? Did women there consider themselves the equals of men in every sense of the word? He had heard that this was so, but he had found it hard to believe.

With a heavy sigh, he said: "Do you have any intentions of getting married in the near future, *señorita*?"

Her eyes widened and she turned to look at him. "Not in the near future, no. Why?"

Rafael moved awkwardly. Such personal questions were alien to him. "I—wondered, that is all, *señorita*." It was growing dark and he was impatient to reach the airport at Puebla. "If—if the child is your niece, what are your intentions?"

Miranda frowned. "My intentions, *señor*?" She shrugged. "I don't know what you mean."

"I phrase myself badly." Rafael braked and changed gear as a handcart suddenly appeared on the road in front of them. "What I mean is—will you take her back to England?"

"Of course." She sounded surprised. "Where else would I take her? I'm her only relative now. Susan—that is, my sister and I have no parents. They've been dead for more than eight years. When Bob—Susan's husband—got a job in Brazil, I was still at college. I hadn't seen either of them for over a year when—when I had news that they were missing."

"I see." Rafael paused. "So you may find it —difficult to cope with a child?"

Miranda half turned in her seat towards him. "Do you really care, *señor*...?"

Rafael stiffened. That she should ask *him* that! He made a dismissing movement of his shoulders. "Of course it is the duty of anyone to care, *señorita*. The child is young—impressionable. She needs a firm hand as well as a secure background. She needs good food and clothing, someone to whom she may turn in times of trouble, someone who is always there in the background, always ready to offer assistance and advice."

Miranda traced the grain in the leather at the back of his seat with a careless finger. "And don't you think I can provide these things? Is that what you're getting at?"

"I did not say that, *señorita*. But you are young, you have your own life to lead. What place in it would there be for an orphaned eight-year-old girl?"

She swung round in her seat. "I get the feeling you're trying to tell me something, *señor*," she remarked coldly.

Rafael sighed, wishing for the umpteenth time that he had not agreed to become a part of this impossible situation. "It is simply that my brother is concerned for the child's welfare, *señorita*," he stated flatly. "Is it not natural that this should be so. These past weeks she has been—how shall I say?—the centre of attention."

"But she doesn't remember who she is, does she?" Miranda retorted. "How do you think she'll feel when she discovers that her—her parents are dead?"

"That is impossible to answer, of course."

"Of course." She hunched her shoulders. "But don't you think that for a child of Lucy's age, having someone she knows, someone she *really* knows, to care for her, is more important in the immediate term than anything else?"

"Perhaps so, *señorita*."

"But you're not sure, are you?" She tossed her head impatiently. "I'm beginning to think I know why your brother did not come to meet me himself. He wanted you to plead his case—didn't he? Be his advocate! But why? What does Lucy mean to him?"

Rafael saw the lights of Puebla looming ahead of them with some relief. "We will complete our journey by helicopter, *señorita*," he stated stiffly. "Then you will meet my brother and judge for yourself what his motives may be."

At the airport, formalities were soon dealt with, and

35

he led the way to that quieter corner of the airfield where a silver and blue helicopter glinted in the dull lights. Miranda had said nothing since leaving the car, and if she was surprised to find herself expected to complete the journey in a helicopter she made no demur. It was Rafael who found himself growing increasingly disturbed and after securing her in the seat beside him he fastened his own straps with impatient fingers. He should never have come on this mission. If anything he had prejudiced the girl against Juan by his own carelessness.

In the air he felt a little more relaxed. Flying, whether in the helicopter or in the monoplane also owned by the estate, always relaxed him. His father had been a keen pilot and some of Rafael's earliest memories were of being taken up in an aeroplane and subjected to the kind of aerobatics calculated to shake the hardest nerves. But Rafael had loved it, and by the time he was fourteen he could handle a plane almost as well as his father. Of course, his mother had not known, not then, but as soon as he was old enough to hold a licence it had become one of his greatest pleasures. A pleasure he had denied himself of late.

Now as he turned the helicopter towards the valley of the Lima, he reflected that he could afford to be pleasant to the girl when in a little over an hour she would no longer be his responsibility. He knew the terrain like the back of his hand, and felt he could have flown the chopper in blindfold. He glanced towards his passenger and saw her taut features revealed in the diffused lighting from the instrument panel. He felt a sense of remorse. He had been cold and unyielding, totally unlike his normal self. It was not her fault that he instinctively recoiled from her easy familiarity. What must she be thinking of him?

He shook his head. Juan should not be too disappointed. After all, he, too, had been expecting an older woman. What he would say when he confronted this emancipated specimen of womanhood might be interesting to hear. But something had to be said now and Rafael sought for suitable words.

"No one has any intention of trying to—take your niece—if indeed the child is your niece—away from you, *señorita*," he averred at last.

She looked sideways at him. "No one could."

Her determination was irritating. She was obviously unaware of the power of the Cueras family if she imagined her words would carry much weight here.

"I—should not take that attitude, *señorita*," he replied quietly. "You are not in England now."

"Are you threatening me, *señor*?" she demanded incredulously, and his knuckles showed white through the skin of his hands.

"No, *señorita*, I am not threatening you. I am merely offering sound advice."

She directed her attention towards him. "And what do you do, *señor*? Do you work for your brother on this estate Father Esteban mentioned in his letters? Are you working for him now?"

Rafael could not remember feeling so angry for a very long time. "No," he managed, through clenched teeth. "I do not *work* for my brother, *señorita*. I have no connection with the estate."

"I see."

But she was puzzled. He sensed that. However he had no intention of enlightening her further. She would learn soon enough no doubt. But not from him. He did not altogether understand his antipathy towards the girl, but he wanted nothing more to do with her.

Thereafter there was silence between them. They flew in over the mountain ranges, dropping low into the valley where lights pricked the gloom below them. A fugitive moon slid from behind clouds long enough to illuminate the grey walls of the Hacienda Cueras, but then they fell behind them as the helicopter dropped down to the valley floor where a narrow airstrip flanked by adobe buildings provided a necessary landing area. As they landed Miranda looked curiously about her, probably noticing the lack of formal buildings.

"Is this it?" she asked, and he nodded.

"This is it, *señorita*," he agreed coolly, thrusting back the sliding perspex door as the propellers slowed to a stop. "Only a short journey in a Landrover and you will be at the Hacienda Cueras."

"Oh, but—" Miranda broke off. "I thought Lucy was staying at the mission with Father Esteban."

"She is, *señorita*. But the mission is small, accommodation is limited. My brother insists you accept his hospitality. Besides, it would not be advisable to upset the child at this time of night."

He thought she was about to refuse, but although her mobile mouth tightened she tossed back her hair with a careless hand and bent to unfasten her safety harness. He offered her his hand to climb out, and after a moment's hesitation she took it, her fingers slim and cool in his. It was the first time he had touched her, and he could tell from the way her eyes darted to his face that she was not unaware of him. But he withdrew his hand as soon as he could and turned away with relief to speak to Gerardo Sanchez, the mechanic, who lived in one of the adobe buildings. They spoke in a swift patois, a mixture of Mexican and the native Nahuatlan, which successfully excluded Miranda. All the same, Rafael was conscious of her standing there, behind him, slim and elegant, in spite of her casual attire, looking about her with interested eyes.

It was quite cold now, and after a moment he dismissed Gerardo and turned back to her.

"Come," he said. "The Landrover is waiting, and so, too, is my brother. Gerardo tells me that he did not get my message last evening informing him that your plane had been delayed."

He set off across the tarmac and she fell into step beside him. "What do you mean?" she asked in surprise. "Didn't you telephone."

Rafael cast her an impatient look. "There are no telephones in the high valleys of the Chiapas, *señorita.*" He shrugged. "No doubt both he and my mother have convinced themselves by now that I have either run the Mustang off the highway, or crashed the helicopter!"

Miranda bit her lip, looking at him anxiously, and in the fleeting light of the moon she saw the amusement touching his mouth. She smiled suddenly, and a gulp of laughter escaped her.

"It is not funny," he asserted, straightening his lips, but her smile was infectious and in spite of himself he grinned back.

"You look so much nicer when you smile," she exclaimed impulsively, and he was glad that they had reached the Landrover and thus was not obliged to make any response.

Gerardo slung the luggage into the back and raised his hand in farewell, and then they bumped off across the grassy sward that led to the track. The scent of pine and underbrush filled the air, mingling with the baser scents of earth and humanity. Rafael handled the Landrover expertly, accelerating as they left the airstrip behind and began the ascent into the foothills.

The Hacienda Cueras looked particularly beautiful in the light cast from its many windows, and Miranda exclaimed at the mosaic tiling on the stone fountain in the forecourt which he usually took for granted. He found the sound of its falling waters cooling on a hot afternoon, but that was all.

He had hardly stopped the vehicle before the shallow steps which led up to the shadowed portico when the mesh door was opened and his mother stood silhouetted against the light beyond. She spread her hands welcomingly and came hurrying down the steps towards him as he stepped from the Landrover.

"Rafael! Oh, *Rafael!*" she exclaimed weakly. "*Dios gracias, estas aqui! De donde—*"

"*No ahora,* Madrecita," said Rafael soothingly. "*Estoy seguro.*" He took her clinging arms from around his neck, glancing back to where Miranda Lord was just getting out of the Landrover. "*Esta* Miss Lord, Madrecita. Miss Miranda Lord."

Doña Isabella's eyes widened in surprise as she took in the informally clad girl behind him. "This is—the child's aunt from England?" she asked in that language.

Rafael hid his amusement at his mother's astonishment. If he had been surprised, his mother was shocked.

"That is correct," he agreed. "Miss Lord, this is my mother, Doña Isabella Cueras."

Miranda held out her hand and Doña Isabella shook it politely, but her expression was far from welcoming. However, politeness was an inbred instinct, and she managed to say: "I hope you had a good journey, *señorita.*"

Miranda nodded. "Reasonably so. The flight was delayed twenty-four hours in Jamaica through engine trouble. I'm sorry if you've been worried, but your son did send a message."

Doña Isabella's dark eyes turned to her son. "Is this so, Rafael?"

"Of course. Gerardo told me you did not receive it."

Doña Isabella made an impatient sound. "No, we did not. We have been most concerned about you, Rafael. And—and about you, too, of course, *señorita.*" This last was clearly an afterthought.

Rafael leaned into the back of the Landrover and hauled out Miranda's belongings. "Well, it is over now. We are arrived safely. And if you will excuse me, there are matters which require my immediate attention."

Miranda stared at him in dismay. "You're—leaving?"

Rafael made her a slight bow. "I am afraid so. As I told you, *señorita*, I do not live at the hacienda. My mother will take care of you and presently my brother will show himself."

She made a helpless gesture. "But—"

Rafael turned away from the appeal in her eyes and ignoring his mother's reproachful: "Rafael!" he climbed back into the Landrover. *"Adios, amigos. Nos hablaremos pronto. Adios!"*

CHAPTER THREE

MIRANDA had never slept between silk sheets before. Indeed, she had scarcely been aware that such luxuries existed, born as she had been into an ordinary household whose budget only ran to flannelette in winter and cotton in summer. Of course, after her parents had been killed there had been no household to speak of; her sister, Susan, was already married and as Miranda herself had been only fourteen and still at school at the time she had had little choice but to make her home with them. It had not been an altogether satisfactory arrangement. She and Susan had vastly different temperaments and Susan's jealousy over the younger girl's popularity caused a great deal of dissention. In addition to which, Lucy had just appeared on the scene, and as Susan chose to neglect herself in favour of the child, her husband turned more and more towards Miranda. Miranda didn't encourage him, but she was naturally friendly with everyone and it wasn't until it was too late that she defined his intentions. It was perhaps fortunate for all concerned that she was able to leave school and go on to college, and in the holidays she always managed to get work that provided living accommodation. But it was still a shock when they went missing, although she did not miss them as much as she would have done had they always been a closely knit family.

Now Miranda moved her legs lazily beneath the silken coverings and wondered however she was going to sleep with so many disturbing thoughts on her mind.

Her room, to which she had been shown after Rafael Cueras's departure, was the most beautiful room she had ever seen. The walls were hung with caramel silk, the wide bed and long windows were draped with apricot brocade, and there was a long fitted unit in a dark wood which she felt sure was not just a veneer. There was a circle of fluffy white carpet on the floor and around its edges the wood gleamed from frequent polishings. Adjoining this magnificent apartment was an equally magnificent bathroom whose appointments, while being a little outdated, were nevertheless built on the grand scale. The whole building exuded luxury and elegance and was far more impressive than anything she had expected. As for the owner, Juan Cueras—well, he was apt to be overshadowed, in her mind at least, by his brother, Rafael.

She sighed and rolled on to her back. *Don Juan!* She said the words deliberately. She had never expected to meet an actual Don Juan in the flesh, although the living being had been far different from the legend. His brother would have suited the name more appropriately. Rafael!

She punched the soft pillows impatiently. Why did her thoughts turn persistently to that man? He had not even treated her with common courtesy. He had behaved as if she were guilty of some crime in coming here to find her niece. All the same, he had been attractive, she conceded moodily, and it was the first time in her young life that any man had treated her with such indifference. His brother had treated her altogether differently, so why didn't she think of him more favourably?

After Rafael had driven away, Doña Isabella had escorted her into the hacienda. She, like her son, did not appear to look with favour on his visitor from England, but she was infinitely more polite. She suggested that Miranda was tired and that perhaps it would be as well if she left all further introductions until the morning. She proposed that Miranda should be shown to her room, offered some food, and then retire for the night.

And, indeed, that prospect was not altogether displeasing to Miranda herself. She was tired, and she guessed that Doña Isabella, like Rafael, had expected someone older and therefore needed time to make the adjustment. But at that moment, a door to their left opened and a man emerged who could only be Juan Cueras. She saw the resemblance to Rafael at once, only this man was more swarthy, thicker set, and only about her own height.

"Qué?" he exclaimed in surprise when he saw them. *"Donde es* Rafael?" And then a curious smile spread over his face. "I hear a vehicle, Mama," he went on in English. "Is Rafael home?"

His mother's lips tightened. "Rafael has been and gone, Juan. Miss—Miss Lord's plane was delayed in Jamaica. That was why he did not come home last night." She bit into her lower lip. "Er—this is my son, *señorita*—Don Juan Cueras."

Miranda responded to his warm smile. "How do you do, *señor*. I'm very grateful to you for offering me your hospitality."

Juan Cueras surveyed her appraisingly, and then shook his head. "You are the aunt of the child?" He chuckled. "But no—you are little more than a child yourself, *señorita*."

His words were similar to those used by his brother, but his intonation was vastly different. It seemed that at least one person did not object to her presence here in Guadalima, and of all of them he perhaps had the most reason.

Doña Isabella was less enthusiastic. "I was just suggesting that Miss Lord might prefer to go at once to her room, Juan," she remarked insistently. "I have no doubt that she is tired, and all discussions concerning her reasons for being in the valley can be conducted so much less emotionally in the light of morning."

Juan looked speculatively at Miranda. "And is this your wish, too, Miss Lord?"

44

"I—" Miranda had been at a loss to know what to reply. "I am tired. I did not sleep well in the hotel in Kingston."

Doña Isabella looked relieved. "It is so, then. I will have Jezebel show you to your room. Everything is prepared. Jezebel is the housekeeper here, *señorita*. She will ensure that you have everything you need."

"You're very kind." Miranda managed a smile of thanks, but when his mother went to summon the housekeeper, Juan Cueras lingered.

"Tell me, Miss Lord," he intoned quietly, "did my brother tell you how—*me gusta*—er—I—I care for the *niña*? Lucy, is it not?"

Miranda relaxed. "Of course. And I should thank you for what you've done for her. Father Esteban has written and told me how often you've visited her—how often she had visited you here."

Juan's swarthy features expanded. "*No tanto. Soy su amigo*—we are friends, *si*?"

"I'm sure your attention has made everything so much easier for her," insisted Miranda, looking about her with interest. "And this beautiful old house—she must love coming here"

Juan was making some deprecatory comment when his mother returned accompanied by an elderly Indian woman whom Miranda assumed must be the housekeeper, Jezebel. It was an unlikely name for such a wizened old creature, but her eyes were sharp and appraising and Miranda guessed they missed nothing.

"You will show Señorita Lord to her room and provide her with a light meal, Jezebel," Doña Isabella was saying as they neared the others, and Jezebel was nodding.

"*Si, señora.*" Continuing to stare at the newcomer, she said: "You come—*por favor*?"

"Yes, go with Jezebel," directed Doña Isabella, linking hands on which glinted a veritable fortune in

45

diamonds. "She will take good care of you. We will meet again in the morning."

"Yes. Yes, thank you." Miranda glanced awkwardly at Juan. "Goodnight then—Doña Isabella; *señor*."

She could not bring herself to say Don Juan, although she supposed that this was his usual appellation. However, he seemed to notice nothing amiss and presently she was walking behind Jezebel up a baroque staircase followed at some distance by one of the menservants carrying her case and haversack.

She sighed now. If she didn't go to sleep soon she would be too tired to drag herself out of bed in the morning. But everything was so strange, so uncannily quiet after the sounds of traffic that constantly created noise beneath the windows of her small flat in Chelsea. It was strange to think that life was still going on as usual beneath those windows half across the world, and that one of the typists from the pool would be taking short-hand from David Hallam possibly at this very moment.

David had not wanted her to come to Guadalima to identify her niece. He valued her services too highly as his secretary to appreciate the disruption her departure had caused. He had said it would have been much more sensible to have the child flown to England for identification as that was where she was going to live. But then David was a cold fish, and had never fully recovered from her rejection of his marriage proposal four months ago.

It had been at the time when her sister and brother-in-law had first gone missing, and no doubt he had imagined she would welcome his offer with open arms. But he had been mistaken. Much as she liked David, much as she was aware of his fair good looks, much as she knew that the other girls in the office envied her position as his private secretary, she had no illusions about her own feelings. She couldn't picture herself married to David Hallam. She couldn't see herself hostessing his little dinner parties, taking care of his service flat, bringing up a clutch of children exactly like him in every way. He was too correct, too—sedate. His shirts were always pristine white, his ties were never crooked, his hair was never overly long. In short he was the glossy magazine's idea of the successful young businessman, and he never forgot it. Miranda felt sure that had she accepted him he would have attempted to mould her into the successful young businessman's wife, and she simply wasn't interested. It wasn't that she was careless with her own appearance. She liked wearing casual clothes, but she equally enjoyed putting on pretty dresses and being absurdly feminine. However, a mortgaged detached on a suburban estate was not her idea of what life was all about, although she had to admit that she liked the company of men and some day would want a home and children of her own.

Thinking of marriage brought her thoughts back to the conversation she had had with Rafael Cueras on their way to the airport at Puebla. He had been most determined in his negation of her question about his own marriage. She wondered why. Had some woman jilted him in the past—or was he merely a woman-hater? The former seemed unlikely, the latter equally so. He was so arrogantly masculine himself, he could not possibly dislike the opposite sex. And yet he had seemed totally unmoved by her personality, and she moved restlessly when she recalled how coolly he had treated her.

She turned on to her stomach, feeling the silken sheets like a caress against her bare skin. Somehow cotton pyjamas had seemed an unsuitable accoutrement to these exquisite appointments, and besides, after the tossing and turning she had done she felt hot, her skin sticky.

Tomorrow, she thought determinedly, she would think about tomorrow, not today. And then perhaps she might find it easier to relax.

*　　*　　*

She must eventually have slept, because when she opened her eyes it was to the sound of someone drawing back her curtains, throwing wide the shutters of her windows. She blinked, rolling on to her back, drawing the sheet which was her only covering with her. A young Indian girl was turning from the windows, and a smile spread over her rather flat features when she saw that Miranda was awake.

"*Buenos dias, señorita,*" she greeted her cheerfully. "*Esta hambre?*"

Miranda struggled up on to her elbows, holding the sheet firmly against her breasts. "Er—I'm afraid I don't speak Spanish," she said, shaking her head. "*No comprende!*" Were they the right words? "Do you speak English?"

The girl frowned. "*Inglés, señorita?* Ah, *no.*"

Miranda sighed. "Never mind."

"*Qué?*" The girl stared at her anxiously, clearly thinking that something was wrong, and Miranda shook her head again, smiling this time.

"It's not important," she said, hoping her tone would convey her feelings, and then became aware of a delicious aroma of roasted coffee assailing her nostrils. She looked round in surprise to find a tray resting on her bedside table. A closer investigation revealed a jug of freshly squeezed orange juice, *croissants* under a perspex cover, a dish containing curls of butter, a jar of apricot conserve and a pot of the aromatic beverage which had first attracted her attention. 'Hmm, how marvellous!" she exclaimed enthusiastically. She looked back at the girl. "Thank you—er—*gracias!*"

"*De nada, señorita.*" The girl smiled again. "*Esta bien, si?*"

"*Si, bien,*" agreed Miranda, draping the sheets sarongwise about her and wriggling across to the table. "*Gracias.*"

"*Gracias, señorita.*"

The girl was obviously loath to leave and seemed to find the shining swathe of red-gold hair which hung in a tangled curtain about Miranda's bare shoulders quite fascinating. She murmured something in her own language, tugging her own skein of black hair impatiently and rubbing at the coppery texture of her skin, and then at last moved to the door. Miranda breathed a sigh of relief when the door closed behind her. She was not accustomed to such intense scrutiny.

As she drank some of the chilled orange juice she looked at her watch. She was surprised to discover it was after nine o'clock. She must have slept more soundly than she had thought.

The informal meal was as delightful as she had expected. The warm *croissants* melted in her mouth and the conserve had whole pieces of apricot to prove its authenticity. She drank several cups of the strong black coffee and then slid out of bed.

Her room was at the side of the house and double doors opened on to a balcony overlooking the sweep of the valley below. She could see a river in the distance, picking its way over stones, while immediately below her a terraced garden was bright with hibiscus and oleander and exotically flowering cacti. There were more familiar blossoms like roses and lilies, sunflowers and poppies, but in this unfamiliar setting they had a curiously alien appearance. Besides, their colours were so much more vivid, their size so much more aggressive.

She breathed deeply and looked away down the valley. She wondered where the mission was situated and whether anyone had told Lucy yet of her arrival. Of course, the child might not be Lucy, but she had grown so used to thinking of her as such that any contingency of a mistake had not really occurred to her. It had to be Lucy, and if Lucy was alive there was always the possibility that Bob and Susan had survived too.

She was about to push open the balcony doors when

awareness of her state of undress brought a mischievous smile to her lips. Somehow she did not think Doña Isabella would approve of her guest attracting the curious eyes of her servants—not to mention her son . . .

She turned instead and entered the bathroom. There was a shower fitment which squirted an erratic flow of water over her heated body and after she had dried herself she tackled her suitcase. She had refused Jezebel's offer of assistance in unpacking its contents the night before, but now she wished she hadn't. She needed a change of clothing and she had soon spilled the contents of the case over the floor. She was buttoning the waistband of a pair of cream levis when there was a knock at her door and she swung round in surprise. "Come in," she called tentatively.

It was the old housekeeper who entered, her shrewd gaze quickly taking in the strewn contents of the suitcase and the rumpled state of the bed.

"*Buenos dias, señorita,*" she said politely. "Inez tells me you wish something?"

Miranda frowned. "Oh, you mean the girl who brought the tray? No. No, actually, I asked her if she spoke English, but she didn't."

"*No, señorita.*"

"Er—your English is very good." Miranda strove for something to say. "And—and the breakfast was—out of this world!"

"Out of this world, *señorita*?" echoed Jezebel, frowning. "What is this?"

Miranda bit her lip. "I'm sorry. It means—heavenly! Marvellous!" She looked round and changed the subject. "As you can see, I've made quite a mess. Is—is Don Juan waiting for me?"

"Waiting for you, *señorita*?"

Miranda couldn't make up her mind whether Jezebel really didn't understand or whether she was being deliberately obtuse. She suspected the latter.

50

"Yes," she explained now. "To take me to see my—the child."

"Oh, Oh, no, *señorita*. Don Juan is taking breakfast on the patio, *por corriente*."

"I see." Miranda picked up a crumpled shirt and began to fold it. "Thank you."

Jezebel put her hands on her hips and gestured at the mess. "You like Jezebel put things away?"

Miranda stared at her in surprise. "Why, no. I can do it."

Jezebel shook her head impatiently. "Is no trouble *señorita*. I do it."

Miranda hesitated. "It's very kind of you, Jezebel, but—"

"Is my job, *señorita*."

Miranda decided not to argue. Besides, now that she was dressed she was eager to see Lucy. It was an exciting prospect after all this time. She pictured the little girl's face when she saw her aunt. She imagined the relief she would see there. How could the child be expected to remember who she was when she was surrounded by strangers, albeit well-meaning strangers? When she saw her aunt, when she recognised her, it would be different.

Leaving Jezebel to bring down the tray, Miranda left her bedroom and walked along the cool tiled corridor which led to the gallery at the head of the flight of stairs. There were portraits on the walls here which she had noticed the night before, but they were dull, unimaginative paintings and she paid little attention to them. In every niche there was a small statue of Christ or the Virgin, impressing upon her most strongly that this was a Catholic household.

Wide doors were open to the terrace at the front of the house, and as she descended the stairs trailing her fingers along the wrought iron balustrade she could smell the perfume from the flowers. In the hall she looked about her doubtfully. This was as far as she had progressed the

51

night before and she had not thought to ask Jezebel how to reach the patio. Of course, it must be at the back of the house, but there were so many archways, so many rooms inviting exploration, and she would hate for Doña Isabella to find her trespassing.

As she hesitated, there were light footsteps behind her and swinging round she came face to face with a girl of about her own age. Small and dark and attractive, she bore the unmistakable Cueras features, and Miranda guessed she must be another member of the family. The girl frowned, however, taking in Miranda's jeans and denim shirt with scarcely concealed distaste. She was wearing well cut jodhpurs and a lemon silk blouse which went well with her darkly tanned skin. Miranda thought inconsequently that it was strange how many shades of colouring there could be in one family. Rafael Cueras's skin had been tanned, but not excessively so, whereas his brother Juan was swarthily Latin. This girl's colouring fell some way between the two.

As she realised that the Mexican girl was not about to rush into speech, Miranda's lips curved upward, and she said: "Good morning. I'm Miranda Lord. You must be some relation of Don Juan. I wonder if you would direct me to the patio."

"I am Carla Cueras," remarked the girl arrogantly. "Juan is my brother. And of course, I know who you are."

This last was said with evident disdain and Miranda curbed the desire to make some equally insolent retort. Instead, she said: "I understand your brother is breakfasting on the patio. I would like to see him."

Carla raised her dark eyebrows. The fact that she was several inches smaller than Miranda did nothing for her temper and she flicked a riding crop impatiently against the side of her boot.

"It is through there," she said offhandedly, indicating an archway to their right.

"Thank you." Miranda's mouth tightened as she turned away and walked through an exquisitely furnished reception area. So that was the sister of the two men she had met yesterday. She wondered if they had any other brothers or sisters, and if so, whether they would be as unfriendly. All in all, Juan's had been the only friendly face she had encountered since arriving in Mexico.

The patio was white-paved and set with colourful garden furniture. Tubs of geraniums and smilax spilled their contents on to the pale stonework of low walls, while beyond a trellis, a rose garden gave off its own inimitable perfume. Beyond the gardens of the hacienda, the verdant slopes of the valley walls gave way to rocks and craggy outcrops where only the hawk and the eagle made their homes.

Juan Cueras was seated at a glass-topped table, smoking a cigar and drinking some of the aromatic coffee Miranda herself had enjoyed earlier. However, at the sound of her approach he looked round and at once sprang to his fee.

"Miss Lòrd!" he exclaimed, with apparent pleasure. "I was just thinking about you." He indicated his chair. "Please to sit. You would like coffee?"

Miranda accepted his chair but refused the coffee. "No, thank you, *señor*—I mean, Don Juan. I—actually I came to find you—to find out how I get to the mission."

"But, *por cierto*, I will take you, *señorita*."

"You will? Miranda's eyes brightened as he seated himself across the table from her. "Is it far?"

"Far? No, *señorita*. At the other end of the valley, that is all."

"Oh, good." Miranda relaxed.

"Did you sleep well, *señorita*."

"Very well, thank you." She excused herself the exaggeration. "This is a beautiful place, isn't it?"

"*Gracias, señorita.*" He inclined his head. "*Esta*

53

hacienda—this estate—is in my family—how you say?—
muchos generacions?"

"Many generations?"

"*Si,* many generations," He smiled. "My English is
not so good."

Miranda laughed. "It's better than my Spanish."

Juan chuckled. "Rafael—my brother—he speaks the
good English, does he not?"

Miranda nodded, but made no comment. She didn't
want to think about Rafael Cueras any more. He had
been responsible for her restlessness the night before
and this morning she had deliberately erased his image
from her mind. But now, with a word, Juan had renewed
that image in all its disturbing force.

"Tell me," Juan was speaking again, and she was
more than willing to be distracted, "you like—er—
aprender hablar español, si?"

Miranda frowned. "To learn Spanish?" she suggested, doubtfully, and relaxed when he clapped his
hands.

"*Bravo!* You see, it is not *dificil.* Rafael will help you.
If he has the time, *naturalmente.*"

"Oh, but really, that's not necessary—I mean—I
couldn't trespass on your brother's time—"

"*Quia!* My brother spends too much time away from
the hacienda, *señorita.* I will speak with him."

"Oh, no—please—"

But Juan was not listening to her. He was staring
broodingly across the patio and his smooth good looks
were shadowed. Then he said: "*Esta deseosa estar con la
niña, señorita?*"

If he imagined her earlier success enabled her to understand everything he said, he was very much mistaken, and Miranda was looking at him helplessly when
a female voice said:

"My brother is asking whether you are eager to see the
child, *señorita.*"

54

Miranda looked up in surprise to see the girl she had spoken to so briefly in the hall leaning against a stone pillar which supported the balcony above. But she had changed her clothes. She was no longer wearing riding gear, but instead, a caftan in shades of blue and green which suited her equally as much as the lemon blouse had done. She had spoken less aggressively too, and Miranda thought she glimpsed sympathy in the lustrous dark eyes. What a transformation!

"Thank you," she said now, smiling her gratitude, and Juan gathered his thoughts and got awkwardly to his feet.

"*Lo siento, señorita*, I am not thinking. My sister, she is our translator, *si*?" He turned to the other girl. "Constancia, have you met our guest?"

Constancia? Miranda was confused. The girl had said her name was Carla!

But now she was speaking. "No, Juan. I did not meet the *señorita* last evening. *Como esta usted, Miss Lord?*"

Miranda took the girl's proffered hand, but her eyes were puzzled. "I thought—that is, didn't we meet just now? In the hall?"

The girl frowned, shaking her head. Then her expression cleared. "Oh, no, *señorita*. That would be my sister, Carla. She must be back from riding."

Miranda made an apologetic gesture. "You're so alike!"

Constancia smiled. When she did so she reminded Miranda forcibly of the man who had brought her to Guadalima, and the knowledge of that unconscious awareness of him on the outer perimeter of her mind irritated her.

"We are twins, *señorita*," Constancia was saying now. "I am the older by fifteen minutes."

"I see." Miranda shook her head. She should have guessed. This girl had a much gentler appearance, a gentler personality, and in that respect she did not resemble her handsome brother. On the contrary, Carla's attitude more closely reflected Rafael's.

Juan straightened. "We go to the mission Constancia," he said. "Why do you not come with us? Your presence might be—helpful, *si*?"

Constancia hesitated. "If Miss Lord does not object."

Miranda made a deprecating movement of her shoulders. "Please come. Lucy—that is, the child knows you. She may not know me."

"Very well. Give me five minutes."

Constancia disappeared indoors again and Miranda got to her feet and walked across the patio to touch the petals of an exotic calla lily. The plant life here had a disturbingly physical presence and Miranda thought of some carnivorous plants she had once seen in a botanical garden back home. Their hairy stalks and smooth rubbery leaves had sent curious shivers of anticipation up her spine, and she could feel that same sensation beginning now.

They drove to the mission in a sleek blue and chrome convertible. Juan himself was at the wheel, although he confessed to preferring being driven. Miranda sat with Constancia in the back.

During the journey, Miranda's attention was captured by the sights and sounds about her. Constancia pointed out the small, flower-decked chapel with its cone-shaped bell tower, the wooden span of a narrow bridge which crossed the waters of the Rio Lima. The river was peaceful today, she told her, but when it was in flood, bridges were swept away and sometimes the valley itself was flooded. In such times, the people fled to the safety of the lower slopes, taking refuge in the chapel, making homes in the barns.

There were occasional groups of adobe dwellings where the estate workers lived, a store, a garage, a doctors' surgery. Once Miranda thought she saw Rafael's Landrover parked outside one of the buildings, but she could not be certain. There seemed little design to the placement of the houses, no rows or streets, but merely a disorganised gathering of habitations without running water or electricity and little sign of sanitation. This last discovery concerned her a little, but she was loath to make any comment which might alienate Juan's friendship. All the same, she was glad when the houses were left behind and they began climbing the track to higher ground where a small white-painted monastery showed unmistakably against the verdant greenery of the hillside.

Constancia pointed towards the building. "There! You can see where the *niña* is staying. It is the Monasterio de San Miguel. Father Esteban *e* Father Domenico—they do much good work for the people of our valley."

"There are only two priests?" Miranda was surprised.

Constancia nodded. "Although it is still called the Monasterio de San Miguel, most of the priests who used to live here died many years ago. Father Esteban is the last surviving member of the original order. Times change. People grow old and die. There is not the people in the valley that there once was. The estate has become mechanised—"

"—and Rafael sends the young people to the city!" declared Juan, with unusual vehemence.

"He tells them of the better living conditions there," agreed Constancia, nodding. "And the money to be earned in the factories is much more attractive than what you pay, Juan."

"*Disparate!* The valley is their home, Constancia."

"They do not all share your obsession for the land, Juan. Do not blame them for seeking to better themselves."

"I do not blame them, Constancia. It is Rafael who makes them—what do you say?—*malcontento*?"

Constancia smiled at Miranda. "As you can see, my

brothers have very different views concerning our people. There are points on both sides. Juan would argue that what one does not have, one does not miss, but Rafael—" she shook her head, "Rafael thinks as a doctor thinks, and he sees only the disease and deprivation. The achievements of our ancestors in wresting this valley from the wilderness and creating an oasis of civilisation and cultivation does not swell the pride in his breast. Rather he sees it as an exploitation of the Indian."

Juan snorted irritably. "Rafael is a *filistino*!" he snapped, but Constancia shook her head.

"He is an idealist, Juan."

"And do you know what this means?"

"*Si*. It means that Rafael believes that man is more important than possessions. He does not admit the primary concept of materialism which is the code we live by, do we not?"

Juan made some uncomplimentary comment in his own language, and then said: "And you are a *conversa, pequeña*?"

Constancia shrugged, running manicured nails along the polished rim of the door at her side of the luxurious vehicle. "I did not say I agreed with him. I am afraid I am too lazy—too fond of material things—to ever fully share his beliefs. But I admire him for them, nevertheless."

Miranda had listened to this interchange in silence, but she had registered every word. What had Constancia meant when she had said Rafael thought like a doctor? Was he a doctor? Was that what he had meant when he said he had no part in the estate? She would have liked to have asked, but in fact it was no concern of hers. And besides, they were nearing the monastery and the prospect of seeing Lucy drove all other thoughts out of her head. Now that they were so near, she was eager to reach their destination, and she refused to admit to a certain cold feeling of unease at the inevitably to be faced possibility that this child might not be Susan's daughter.

The tall stone walls which had gleamed so brilliantly from a distance could now be seen to be crumbling, and the massive iron gates which had once guarded this scholastic retreat from intruders hung on rusted hinges. Above the gateway, an arched bellcot housed a blackened bell which could not have been rung for many a year, while within the courtyard the stone flags were being displaced by the upward thrust of grass and bindweed. The whole place had a melancholy air to which Miranda was instantly sensitive. And then a man and a child emerged from the darkened interior of the building and all other considerations were forgotten.

The man was solemnly garbed in flowing black robes, but above his cassock his homely face beamed. A thatch of thinning overly-long white hair moved in the wind and he constantly endeavoured to smooth it across his balding pate. But it was the child to whom Miranda's eyes were drawn. Small and slender, dressed in a simple cotton frock which Miranda could not remember having seen before, blonde curls framing a piquantly attractive face, there could be no doubt in Miranda's mind that this was Lucy. Although it was eighteen months since she had seen her, there was no mistaking the tip tilted nose, the ofttimes petulant twist of her mouth, which was so like her mother's, the quick, nervous movements.

But if Miranda recognised Lucy, Lucy did not recognise Miranda. After a cursory glance at his companions, it was to Juan that the child sped, holding her arms wide and being swept up into his.

"Tio Juan, Tio Juan!" she shrilled excitedly, hugging him. "Father Esteban told me you were coming. Are you staying? Are you taking me to the hacienda? You will take me with you, won't you, Tio Juan?"

"*Quietud, poca!*" he commanded, but he was laugh-

59

ing, and Miranda thought wryly that it would be most uncharitable of her to suppose that Don Juan was well pleased with this exhibition of his power over the child. All the same, after what Rafael had intimated . . . "We will see, *no?*"

"But you promised!" protested Lucy, pursing her lips sulkily. "You said—"

"*Uno momento, chica!* I bring someone to meet you—"

"Tia Constancia, I know—"

"No, *chica*, not just Tia Constancia. See—there! Do you know who that is?"

He directed the child's attention towards Miranda and she could feel herself stiffening almost without volition. In the uneasy stillness that prevailed after Juan's words she was conscious of every small sound about her—the drugging scrape of the crickets, the chatter of the birds in the branches of a nearby cypress tree, the steadily increasing drone of a vehicle's engine coming up the valley.

Lucy's eyes were painfully intent for a few moments, and then she shrugged indifferently. "Should I?" she asked impatiently.

Don Juan put her slowly to the ground. "Perhaps," he answered, his tones non-committal.

"Of course you should, Lucy!" Miranda made a deliberate reference to the child's name. "Don't you remember me?" She went down on her haunches, beckoning the child towards her. But Lucy made no attempt to leave the security of Juan's side, and worse, there was no sign of recognition in her eyes.

"Why do you call me that?" she demanded scornfully. "*Lucy!* That's not my name. Nobody knows my name."

"I know it, Lucy," insisted Miranda quietly, continuing to hold out her hand, although the coldness inside her refused to be denied now. "It is Lucy. Lucy Carmichael."

"No." Lucy turned startled eyes up to her benefactor. "No—no, it's not—"

"I think you should not frighten her, Miss Lord," said Juan, his hands resting possessively on Lucy's shoulders. "Perhaps this is not the way—"

He broke off abruptly as another man suddenly entered the courtyard, and Miranda remembered vaguely hearing the vehicle in the valley and how it had stopped a few moments ago. Tall and lean, in mud-coloured cotton pants and jacket, with no shirt to hide the muscular broadness of his chest, Rafael Cueras took in the small group that was gathered with a single glance. Then he turned to his brother, and his eyes were hard as he said:

"What is the matter, Juan? Are you afraid the child will remember?"

CHAPTER FOUR

MIRANDA rode back to the hacienda with Rafael in the Landrover. She had not wanted to go with him and she knew with certainty that he had not wanted to take her, but Juan had insisted that it would be easier that way. He had said he needed time to talk to the child, to explain the situation to her—and that it would more easily be achieved without Miranda's presence.

To Miranda herself it was all wrong. She should have been the one to talk to Lucy, to try and explain a little of the circumstances leading up to her presence here, endeavouring to ease the child's immature mind into a state of awareness without making it too painful for her to bear. But instead, Juan had taken command, and although she knew Rafael opposed him there was nothing he could do without creating an impossible state of hostility. Lucy believed in Juan absolutely, she clung to him as a swimmer might cling to a lifeline, and although Miranda could understand this, she could not understand Juan's persistent strengthening of this bond by his attitude. His hold on the child was such that only he could break it, only he could direct Lucy's actions without hysterical reaction. And it seemed he was in no hurry to relinquish that hold . . .

The priest, Father Esteban, was a different proposition. He only wanted what was best for the child, and his attitude towards Miranda had been one of gentle understanding. He had urged her after their introduction to be patient, not to expect too much too soon. Lucy was only eight years old. It was natural that she should need an anchor in these uncertain seas in which she found herself, but that sooner or later nature would take its course and her memory would be restored to her.

Miranda had listened to him intently, but all the while the uncertainty inside herself was growing. How long might nature take to restore the child's memory? How long before she remembered what had happened, that her parents were dead, her true identity? It was four months already since their aircraft went missing. How many more months might elapse before any concrete proof of her identity made itself known to her? And was Miranda expected to remain here for that length of time? *No!* Apart from anything else, she could not afford to do so. David had agreed to giving her two week's leave of absence, but after that . . . And in any case, she could not accept the Cuerases' hospitality for any length of time, and to stay for more than two weeks at an hotel or *pension* was simply beyond her means . . .

A faint sigh escaped her and attracted her companion's attention. "What is it, *señorita*? Is the situation not as straightforward as you imagined?"

"You know it's not!" Miranda gave him an impatient glance. "I just don't know what I am expected to do."

"What do you mean?"

Miranda sighed again. "What if Lucy doesn't remember who I am?"

"You're sure it is Lucy, then?"

"Oh, of course." Miranda brushed a fly from her knee. "It's Lucy, all right. But—" She paused. "Your brother doesn't make it easy."

Rafael's mouth turned down at the corners. "Did you expect he would?"

"I don't know. I don't know what I expected. I suppose the possibility of his becoming attached to the child didn't occur to me. That was what you were trying to tell me on our way here, wasn't it?"

"Among other things," admitted Rafael dryly. "My brother is flattered by the child's devotion. It is a new experience for him. It will pass."

63

"And what am I expected to do in the meantime?" exclaimed Miranda, turning her palms uppermost. "I can't wait around here for Lucy to regain her memory!"

"Why not?"

"Why not?" Miranda was amazed. "*Señor*, I have a job to do back home. I've been given two weeks to settle Lucy's affairs. At least part of that time will be needed to make arrangements when we get back to London."

Rafael shook his head. "An optimistic estimate."

"It's not an estimate. It's an ultimatum! David—that is—Mr Hallam, my employer, demands efficiency."

Rafael looked her way. "You speak of him very familiarly for an employee," he remarked ironically.

"I don't." Miranda uttered an exasperated ejaculation. "People are not so—formal back home. In any case, that has nothing to do with it. I couldn't stay here longer than two weeks even if I wanted to."

"Why not?"

Miranda hunched her shoulders. "If you must know, I couldn't afford to do so."

Rafael frowned. "Staying at the hacienda will cost you nothing."

"Maybe not. But I can't go on staying there!"

"At the risk of repeating myself yet again—why not? You seem to be making a great many difficulties out of what seems to me to be a perfectly simple situation."

Miranda gasped. "It's easy for you to say that. Your brother may not see it that way."

"May not see what that way?"

"My staying at the hacienda. As you told me, you have no part of it. Your brother owns the estate."

"Ah!" Rafael's fingers tightened around the steering wheel. "*Bien*—nominally this is so."

"Nominally?"

"It is a complicated affair, *señorita*. Sufficient to say that if I wish you to stay at the hacienda, have no fear, my brother will not object."

Miranda shook her head. "I have to get back."

"With—or without your niece?"

Miranda's eyes clouded. "You think your brother would keep her here?"

"Your tone implies—against her will. But that might not be so. If—Lucy—does not regain her memory, I venture to state that she will not wish to leave. At least, not yet."

Miranda pressed her lips tightly together to prevent them from trembling. "Oh, what a *mess*!"

"A mess, *señorita*? At least Lucy is happy. That should mean something to you."

Miranda turned her head away and stared through the open window. "That's very easy for you to say, isn't it?" She scarcely saw the fields of waving corn that flanked the narrow track. "But what am I going to do?"

Rafael swung the wheel to avoid a deep pothole and moved his shoulders thoughtfully. "Dare I venture to suggest that you are being a little—how do you say?— precipitate, *no*? It is too soon to start worrying about what is to happen. The child does not remember you. You must begin to know her all over again."

Miranda shook her head. "And how long do you expect this will take? How long before Lucy will give up—all this?" She gestured towards the blue sky above them, the increasing heat of the sun which was already causing her shirt to cling to her shoulder blades.

Rafael shrugged. "Who knows?"

"I could take her anyway."

"You could," agreed Rafael quietly. "But I somehow do not think you will force her to go with you. What kind of beginning would that be for your life together?"

"You're so—so practical, aren't you?" she declared, turning to stare at him mutinously. "But you're not involved, are you? What a pity Lucy isn't in your care!"

Rafael slowed as a small herd of cattle on the track in front of them blocked their passage. The herdsman waved and shouted a greeting to him, and Rafael leaned out of the window as they passed, speaking in the native *patois* which Miranda found totally incomprehensible. Then, as the cattle fell behind them, he said: "Why should you suppose I would be any more willing to relinquish my guardianship of the child than my brother, *señorita*?"

Miranda looked down at her hands. She didn't honestly know why she thought that herself. The impression Rafael had deliberately created had not been a favourable one and yet, for some inexplicable reason, she believed he was an honourable man, a man who could not use devious means to win a child's affection.

"I don't know," she said at last. Then she looked up. "Why is your brother doing this? He must know that sooner or later Lucy's memory will return."

Rafael sighed. "I cannot answer for my brother, *señorita*. Perhaps you should ask him."

Miranda returned to her contemplation of her hands. "I—I don't know how. Oh, God, I wish I knew what to do—I wish—I wish there was someone . . ."

She could feel tears smarting on the back of her eyes and brushed her hand across her cheek impatiently. Self-pity was going to get her nowhere. What was the matter with her? She had always considered herself capable of coping with any emergency—free, independent, any man's equal. And now suddenly she felt as helpless as a babe in arms.

They were approaching the collection of houses which, as it encompassed the store and doctor's surgery, seemed the main street of the community. To Miranda's surprise, Rafael turned the Landrover off the track and wound his way between the shabby dwellings with the expertise of long use. Children squatting, half-naked, in the mud, squealed as he passed and women stopped what they were doing to raise a hand in greeting. It seemed obvious that Rafael was well known and well

66

liked here, although, thought Miranda rather cynically, it was only natural that as he was the brother of the *patron* it should be so. Even so, she wondered where he was taking her and speculated upon Juan's reactions when he discovered they had not followed him more closely. The sleek convertible with Juan at the wheel, Lucy bouncing excitedly on the seat beside him, had left the monastery ahead of the Landrover as Rafael had lingered to talk to Father Esteban.

Through the open doors of the houses she glimpsed the bare interiors and her lips tightened when she recalled the exquisite elegance of the Hacienda Cueras. So great a distinction in so small a community was all wrong. But, of course, she said nothing.

They emerged from the houses on a sloping lip of land overlooking the river. The air was much fresher here, although the sight of an open sewer running down into the surging waters was disturbing. Standing squarely on the slope was a small stone building, with a sloping tiled roof. White shutters stood wide from windows without glass, and a creeper with small purple flowers which reminded Miranda of morning glory clung round the doorway. Rafael accelerated up to the house and then cut his engine.

Miranda turned to look at him in surprise, and he flexed his shoulder muscles wearily, unconsciously drawing her attention to the silver cross on its slender chain resting among the curls of dark hair on his chest. Then, as though becoming aware of her scrutiny and resenting it, he slid from his seat, saying abruptly: "Come! I will provide you with some coffee, *señorita*."

"This is your house!"

Miranda was incredulous, but she wished she had not shown such astonishment when he replied curtly: "Yes, *señorita*. This is where I live while I am here. It is not so impressive as the hacienda, I know, but it is clean and it suits me very well."

Miranda scrambled out of the Landrover. "I—I didn't mean—that is—I think it's delightful!" she exclaimed uncomfortably.

Rafael made no comment but went ahead of her up the path to the door. Inside, a stone-flagged passage ran from front to back, with several doors opening from it. It was cool inside after the heat of the day, and there was a lingering scent of ground coffee.

Rafael opened a door to their right as they entered and showed her into a small sitting room. The floor here had been tempered by the strewing of several rugs, and there was a comfortable settee, a desk, and an occasional table.

"If you will please sit, I shall not be a moment," he suggested politely, and Miranda couldn't think of anything else to say at that moment.

However, after he had left her, she moved about the room restlessly, and presently opened the door into the corridor and looked out. Perhaps she ought to have offered to make the coffee for him, she thought, impatient with herself for not thinking of it before. But did he live here alone, or did someone share it with him? She remembered again what Constancia had said about Rafael thinking like a doctor. Was he a doctor? Was this perhaps his surgery as well as his home? And what had he meant by saying that this was where he lived when he was here? Where else did he live? Not at the hacienda, she was sure of that.

Leaving the sitting room door ajar, she walked tentatively along the passage. The other doors were all closed except for one at the end, but when she peeped in here she found it was the kitchen and Rafael was heating a percolator on a small gas stove.

"Can I do anything to help?" she asked, and he looked round at her, almost irritably, she thought. But why? He had brought her here. She hadn't asked to come.

"No. No. I can manage, *señorita*," he refused curtly. "It is almost ready."

Miranda lingered. She could sense that she was not welcome, but as she couldn't understand why she didn't see why she should scuttle away like a chastised mouse.

"Do you live here alone?" she asked, running her fingers over the roughened surface of a scrubbed wooden table that clearly served the dual purpose of working and eating space.

Rafael nodded. "More or less."

"What does that mean?"

He turned off the percolator as it began to bubble. "Sometimes Doctor Rodrigues will leave a patient in my care. I have rooms to spare."

Miranda looked at him through her lashes. "And are you a doctor?"

He looked up. "I am entitled to put M.D. after my name, if that is what you mean, *señorita*."

Miranda didn't understand this ambiguous remark and was silent for a moment as she watched him pouring strong black coffee into thick white beakers.

"I regret I cannot offer you bone china," he commented, passing her a beaker and indicating the jug of milk and bowl of sugar on the table. "Please—help yourself."

Miranda spooned sugar into her cup and stirred it. "This is fine," she said, forcing a polite smile.

"Shall we go back to the lounge, *señorita*?" he suggested, inclining his head towards the door, and she hesitated for a moment before saying:

"There's no need." She sat down on the wooden stool beside the table. "This is fine."

She sensed his impatience at her perversity, but short of ordering her out of the kitchen there was nothing he could do. Instead, he rested his back against the white stone sink and raised his beaker of coffee to his lips. Miranda watched him surreptitiously and wondered at her own curiosity about him. He was attractive, it was true, but she had known many more handsome men. So what was it about him that aroused this awareness of his physical presence? Why were her eyes continually drawn to his unsmiling dark face, to the lean hardness of his body? The muscles of his thighs were taut beneath the close-fitting cotton trousers, his legs long and powerful. She looked down into her beaker. She wondered what he would do if showed that she found him attractive. It might be amusing to find out. She had never known a man so emotionally unmoved by her personality.

Then she bit hard into her lower lip. What was she thinking about? She wasn't here to indulge in promiscuous flirtations with dark-eyed Mexicans who might indeed prove more than she could handle. She was here to gain Lucy's confidence—to bring her back to her own country.

Following this line of thought, she said: "So your opinion, so far as Lucy is concerned, is that I should wait a few days before making any decision?"

Rafael was drinking from his cup, his head tipped back, and her eyes followed the moving line of muscles in his throat as they expanded and contracted in swallowing. Then he lowered the cup and looked across at her. "Naturally it is up to you to decide what you think is best, *señorita*."

Miranda felt exasperated. "Must you continually call me that? she exclaimed. "*Señorita!* Why can't you call me Miranda?"

"Does my brother call you—Miranda, *señorita*?" he enquired gravely, and her name on his lips had a curiously alien quality about it.

"No, of course not," she snapped. "I hardly know your brother."

"You hardly know me, *señorita*."

She supposed in all honesty that that was true, and yet

70

for some reason her relationship with Rafael *was* different from the contact she had had with Juan. She didn't altogether understand why, but already she was beginning to rely on Rafael.

"I—I feel as though I do know you," she protested slowly. "I—I can't explain exactly, but—well, it's different with you somehow."

She was shocked by the grimness in Rafael's expression which her words provoked. "You are mistaken, *seōrita*," he assured her coldly. "Our association is in no way—different! On the contrary, it is my brother to whom you should be expressing your doubts and uncertainties, not me!" He slammed his beaker down on the draining board next to the sink. "And now, if you have finished—"

"I haven't." Miranda pursed her lips indignantly. "And I don't know why you should get so steamed up just because I paid you what I thought would have been taken as a compliment."

Rafael turned his back on her, tapping his thigh with impatient fingers. "I do not need your compliments, *señorita*."

Miranda's fingers trembled as they gripped her cup. "Then I don't know why you brought me here if you find my company so distasteful!" she declared tremulously.

"If you must know, I felt sorry for you," stated Rafael harshly, and she caught her breath.

"Oh—oh, all right!" She swallowed the remainder of her coffee at a gulp and almost burnt her mouth in the process. "I'm finished. Let us go, by all means."

Rafael turned then, his features composed, long lashes hiding the expression in his eyes, concealing his feelings which she knew to be far from composed. He gestured towards the door and she went ahead of him along the stone passage and out into the heat of the day.

The journey to the hacienda was completed in silence. but when he brought the Landrover to a halt at the foot

71

of the shallow steps leading up to the terrace, she turned to him impulsively and said: "Thank you for the coffee anyway. I did enjoy it. And I liked your house."

Rafael's eyes darkened as they rested on her warm beauty, lingering for a tantalising moment on the parted softness of her mouth. But the hardness was in his voice as he said:

"*De nada, señorita*. It was nothing."

He would have gone then, but unexpectedly his mother's voice stopped him. "Rafael, Rafael, *uno momento! Con te quiero hablar* . . ."

Miranda stepped away from the Landrover as Doña Isabella came regally down the steps towards them. However, she scarcely spared a glance for the girl but went straight to the vehicle, speaking in remonstrative tones to her son. Miranda had no idea what she was saying, but it was obvious that something had annoyed the older woman, and feeling slightly *de trop* she began to climb the steps to the terrace.

"Do not go, *señorita*. I wish to speak to you."

Miranda turned in surprise to find that Doña Isabella was addressing her now. "Yes, Doña Isabella?" she murmured politely, pausing halfway up the steps.

Rafael thrust open the door of the Landrover and climbed out. "Madrecita, you must not interfere," he commanded forcibly.

Doña Isabella looked at him reproachfully. "Rafael, this has gone far enough. Juan is besotted with the child. Miss Lord must take her back to England, at once!"

Miranda looked at each of them in turn, her brows drawn together above troubled eyes. "Doña Isabella, that's what I want to do—" she was beginning, when Rafael interrupted her.

"*Senorita*, my mother knows quite well that it would be cruel to separate the child from the small things which have become familiar to her, to eject her into a society of which she has no recollection."

72

"And what do you suggest, Rafael?" exclaimed Doña Isabella tremulously.

"I suggest that you give Miss Lord time to get to know her niece—to gain her confidence—to talk with her about her parents," replied Rafael.

Doña Isabella uttered an impatient sound. "How long will such an undertaking last? How can Miss Lord get to know her niece here when Juan monopolises her attention?"

Rafael sighed. "You are making difficulties, *madre mia*. There is no urgency—at least—" his glance flickered over Miranda, "—at least so far as we are concerned, is there?"

Doña Isabella's lips tightened. "Miss Lord is to stay at the hacienda, then?"

Rafael raised his eyes heavenward. "Where else would she stay?"

"I see."

Miranda felt terrible. "If there is somewhere else—" she ventured, but Rafael turned such cold eyes on her tentative suggestion that she fell silent.

"You will stay at the hacienda, *señorita*," he stated uncompromisingly. "Is this not so, Madre?"

Doña Isabella looked at her son strangely. "You are giving orders, Rafael?" she questioned quietly, and Miranda was astonished by the spasm of emotion which twisted his face.

"*Si. Si,*" he muttered, turning away to grasp the frame of the Landrover. "I must go. I promised Rodrigues I would go and see the child of Calero."

"And what did you promise me, Rafael?" asked his mother emotively, pressing a scrap of lace to her lips.

Rafael turned to look at her with tortured eyes. "I—I—what do you want of me?"

Doña Isabella held up her head, and Miranda wished she could disappear off the face of the earth. "I want for you to come to the hacienda, Rafael. You promised you

73

would come. Do I warrant none of your time?"

Rafael swung himself up into the driving seat of the Landrover. "It is impossible today," he exclaimed, turning the ignition.

"Tomorrow, then." His mother was insistent. "Come to dinner." She glanced round at Miranda. "I am sure Miss Lord will be glad to see you."

Rafael slammed the vehicle into gear. "*Esta bien*. I will come to dinner," he agreed briefly, and without any word of farewell he drove away.

After he had gone there was an awkward silence, and feeling she had to say something, Miranda spread her hands. "I don't know how to thank you for allowing me to stay here, Doña Isabella."

The older woman looked up at her and then began to climb the steps heavily. "Do not thank me, *señorita*. I have no authority here. I am permitted to stay here only by the good grace of my son."

Miranda sighed. "Nevertheless, I am grateful. I just wish Lucy had recognised me, that's all."

"So do I, *señorita*." Doña Isabella passed her and continued on up the steps so that Miranda felt obliged to accompany her. When they reached the terrace the older woman turned to her. "Tell me, *señorita*, where did you go with my son?"

Miranda was taken aback. "With your son, Doña Isabella? Why, we went to the monastery to see Lucy, of course."

"Not *Juan*!" Doña Isabella sounded impatient. "Where did you go with Rafael?"

"Oh! Oh, I see." Miranda could feel herself colouring and despised herself for allowing this autocratic woman to intimidate her. "We—we went to his house, *señora*."

"You went to my son's house, *señorita*? You went there *alone* with him?" Doña Isabella sounded horrified. "Why did you go to his house?"

Miranda realised belatedly that to the restricted view

of Doña Isabella such behaviour was reprehensible. "I—we—had coffee," she replied, forcing a smile to her lips. "I—it's a nice house, isn't it? Small, but attractive. And so convenient for his patients, I suppose."

Doña Isabella's lips curled. "I have not seen this house, *señorita*. So far as I am concerned, the hacienda has and will always be my son's home."

Miranda tucked her thumbs awkwardly into the low belt of her jeans. "Yes. Well it's always a—wrench— when a member of one's family leaves home—"

"You do not know what you are talking about, *señorita*." Doña Isabella was barely civil. "This is not England. The Cueras estate is not one of your modest British homes! You can have no conception of what Rafael is giving up!"

Miranda shook her head. "I'm sorry. I was only trying to explain that every mother has to face this problem at some time in their lives. And you do have Juan to run the estate—"

Doña Isabella shook her head vigorously. "You do not understand, as I have said *señorita*." She drew a deep breath. "Excuse me. There are matters requiring my attention."

And with that she walked away along the terrace, a small but elegant figure in the flowing voile gown which complemented the slender lines of her figure.

After she had gone, Miranda herself drew her breath in a trembling gulp. What was all that about? She moved her head uncomprehendingly. So much emotion, so many undercurrents. And she was only conscious of a slight undertow. What might be lurking in deeper waters?

The sound of Lucy's excited voice distracted her. The sound had come from the side of the house and with curiously dragging steps she followed the line of the terrace until she could see them, Lucy, Juan and Constancia, playing a ball game on the stretch of lawn that sloped down to an ornamental pool.

Juan saw her at once and raised his arm to wave to her. *"Hola, señorita!"* he called. "Come. Join us!"

Miranda descended the steps to the lawn with determined effort. It was no use allowing the conflicting emotions around her to influence her judgement. She was here for one reason and one reason only, that of identifying Lucy and ultimately taking her back to England.

CHAPTER FIVE

By the evening of the following day, Miranda had to admit that she had made no progress with Lucy whatsoever. And it was all Juan's fault. Loath as she was to endorse Doña Isabella's opinion of her son's attitude towards the child, she could not ignore his selfish behaviour. Far from encouraging Lucy to talk to her aunt, he continually distracted her, treating Miranda rather like an arbitrator who had come here to decide whether or not to assign the child for adoption. His was a continual demonstration of the child's affection for him, and no one else was allowed to come between.

Not that Lucy made any objections, Miranda had to concede that also. On the contrary, like all children she revelled in constant attention, and Miranda could see that in a very short time she would be completely ruined.

But what could she do? When she spoke to Lucy, Lucy was hostile, regarding her aunt as an intruder, not wanting to hear anything which might involve a change in her status. In a short space of time her immature mind had adapted itself to her circumstances here and Miranda suspected that the longer she stayed the greater the mental block would be. So little was known about the subconscious that it was possible to speculate that the mind might physically reject something as terrifying as a plane crash and the subsequent discovery that her parents were dead. What if the amnesia she was suffering was in a way self-inflicted? She might never recover her memory if she didn't want to do so.

Miranda wished she knew more about amnesia. Father Esteban had offered little explanation of that aspect of the affair in his letters to her. He had told her that the child had been found by a man called Benito Sanchez while on a climbing expedition into the mountains. Sanchez had found the child on a plateau above a narrow ravine, unconscious and suffering from severe exposure. The eventual solution to these circumstances had been that a plane must have crashed into the ravine and that somehow the child had been thrown clear. There were shattered fragments of an aircraft on the plateau which seemed to support this theory, but although a search party had returned to the scene, no further trace of wreckage had been found. Wild though the theory had seemed to Miranda when she had first heard it, the snow had lain thickly on the mountain slopes and it was not entirely inconceivable that it could have cushioned Lucy's fall. Sanchez had brought the child down to the mission at the Monasterio de San Miguel where Father Esteban had cared for her, but it was not until she was able to speak again that it was discovered that she was English and had no apparent recollection of who she might be. It had taken many weeks of investigation to learn that a plane was believed to have crashed in the mountains and that there had been an English family on board.

But now Miranda seated herself before the mirror in the vanity unit and surveyed her appearance. Her hair, which she had washed before taking her bath, was almost dry, and hung in thick strands about her bare shoulders. She was still wrapped in the enormous cream bath-sheet she had draped about her when climbing out of the bath, and she knew that in a few minutes she would have to abandon the reassuring isolation of her bedroom and go downstairs to take dinner with the family. It was not a prospect which filled her with any pleasure, and for the past half hour she had been lying on her bed thinking of anything but the evening ahead.

The previous evening she had dined in her room. She

felt sure it had been a tactical manoeuvre on Doña Isabella's part to demonstrate that although Miranda might be staying at the hacienda, she was not considered a guest. But this evening Juan had invited her to join them and she had not been able to think of any good reason to refuse.

She had had the uncharitable thought that had Lucy still been around even Juan might have had second thoughts, but Lucy was still staying at the monastery and although she had been at the hacienda all day this evening, as last evening, Diaz, the *chofer*, had driven her back across the valley.

Rafael was coming for dinner this evening, too, and that consideration had not been absent from her thoughts when she had wished she might be excused this ordeal. It was not that she disliked him; on the contrary, he disturbed her in a way which she didn't altogether care for, but his attitude towards herself was such that she felt herself to be in a constant state of confusion in his presence. She didn't understand him, of that she was certain, but she also felt that his behaviour was influenced by circumstances of which she had no knowledge.

And there was one other reason why she had no desire to join the family party—Carla.

She had seen the sister of the friendly Constancia twice since that initial encounter yesterday morning and on both occasions Carla had made her dislike of the other girl blatantly obvious. She clearly resented Miranda's presence in the hacienda, and Miranda herself wondered whether the situation would have been any the less fraught if she had turned out to be the middle-aged lady they had expected.

The first of her meetings with Carla had been at lunch the previous day. Miranda would have much preferred to take all her meals in her room, but she could not afford to waste any opportunity offered to talk to Lucy, and she had been delighted to find that her place was beside the child's. No doubt this had been Doña Isabella's doing, but Carla was directly opposite, which rather spoiled things.

Lunch in the Spanish style was taken late and languidly. Wine glasses were kept brimming by attentive servants, and there was much talk and discussion over the meal. They began with tiny spiced pancakes, stuffed with strips of meat and onion and peppers, and Miranda chose to ask Lucy what they were.

Lucy seemed surprised at being asked such a question but she answered: *"Tacos,"* politely enough, pausing in the process of stuffing huge forkfuls into her mouth.

Miranda would have liked to have pointed out that she was not starving and therefore there was no need for such haste, but as no one else seemed to have noticed she was loathe to draw attention to the child in that way. Instead, she said: "We don't have such things back home, do we, Lucy. We eat our pancakes with lemon or syrup. Do you remember? You used to love them."

"Did I?" Lucy was doubtful. "I don't remember, *señorita.*"

Miranda hid her irritation at the formal form of address. "Don't call me *señorita*, Lucy," she protested gently. "You may call me Aunt Miranda—or Auntie— or just Miranda, if you'd rather. But we are related and it seems rather silly for you to behave as though you'd never even seen me before."

"Perhaps she hasn't," remarked Carla then, looking challengingly across the crystal of her wine glass at her adversary. "How do we know you are who you say you are, *señorita?* Have you shown us any proof of your identity?"

"Carla!" It was Doña Isabella who had spoken. "Miss Lord is our guest. You will please to remember that."

"But how do we know she really is my aunt, Tia

Isabella?" Lucy took up the strain, and Miranda was back where she started.

"Look," she said determinedly, bending to pick up her suede shoulder bag from the floor beside her chair. "I have some photographs. Would you like to see them? They're of you—and someone else."

"I do not think is good idea, *señorita*," put in Juan urgently, shaking his head. "Photographs are—how you say?—personal? I think is dangerous to attempt the shocking tactics, *no*?"

Miranda put her bag down again. And it was then that she realised that she was going to get nowhere so long as Juan or some other member of his family was present. Or perhaps that was a little sweeping. Certainly Doña Isabella—and Rafael—would not stand in her way.

Her second confrontation with Carla had occurred at lunchtime today, only this time it had been just before the meal. Miranda had worn a simple lime green cotton shift instead of her usual shirt and jeans. It had been a small concession towards the undoubted distaste Doña Isabella displayed every time she saw Miranda's trousers, but Carla had seen it altogether differently.

"What are you hoping to achieve, *señorita*?" she had hissed in Miranda's ear as they stood waiting for Doña Isabella to appear so that they could all move to the table. The meal was to be served in the high-ceilinged dining room with open French doors on to the terrace.

Now a cool breeze that drifted through these doors fanned Miranda's suddenly heated cheeks. "I don't know what you mean," she said, slanting a glance in Carla's direction.

"Yes, you do, *señorita*. You are thinking how pleasant it is here, and how sensible of Lucy—if that indeed is her name—to decide to stay. Perhaps you are thinking that my brother is—how do you say?—sympathetic to lost causes, *no*? That perhaps with a little persuasion he may be prepared to take responsibility for you also."

81

Miranda gasped. "That's a despicable thing to suggest!"

"Is it?" Carla flicked a careless finger at Miranda's dress. "But this is designed to attract his eyes, is it not? And who knows—you may be successful. My brother, Juan, is not the most astute of men, I think."

To Miranda's relief Doña Isabella appeared at that moment and her swift appraisal of her appearance was hearteningly reassuring. "How attractive you look in a dress, *señorita*," she commented politely. "I must confess to preferring women to look like women."

"Ah, but Miss Lord looks most *femenina* in the *pantalones*, Mama," exclaimed Juan, joining them at the moment and hearing his mother's words. "*Mas*, I agree—she is looking *muy guapa!*"

The conversation was such that Miranda could be forgiven her flushed cheeks, and she couldn't help the small sense of triumph which came from beating Carla at her own game.

But now it was time to dress for dinner, and Miranda rose and tugged the towel free, dropping it in a heap on the carpet. She took clean underwear from a drawer and then extracted the only long dress she had brought with her from the long fitted robe. It was a simple gown of black silk which she had originally bought for a trip to Copenhagen she had made with David, but as it happened she had not worn it after all. She had bought herself a caftan while she was there and had worn that on the evening they had dined with David's business associates.

In consequence, she had a moment's doubt when she slid the dress over her shoulders and allowed it to fall softly to her ankles. Then she relaxed. It looked most suitable. Didn't Spanish and Portuguese women favour black anyway? She shrugged, adjusting the low neckline thoughtfully. The sleeves were long and mediaeval, puffed at the shoulder and narrowing to cling to her forearms. while the skirt was draped and hinted at the slender curve of her legs. It would have to do in any event. She had no alternative.

She hesitated a little longer over her hair. After its washing it was silky thick and looked well spread over the dark material of the gown. During the heat of the day she had secured it at her nape with a tortoiseshell comb, but this evening she decided to leave it loose.

When she was ready to go downstairs she found she was trembling, just a little. It was ridiculous, she knew, but a sudden cold awareness of how alone she was here had swept over her. Perhaps it was the night, she consoled herself, twisting the silver bracelet watch, which had been Susan and Bob's twenty-first birthday present to her eighteen months ago, round her wrist. All the same, she wished she could believe that there was someone here on whom she could depend.

The family were gathered in the main *sala*, an imposing apartment overlooking the front terrace, with magnolia silk walls and a sculpted ceiling. It was furnished with lots of chairs and sofas, also upholstered with silk in shades of mauve and green, and small tables, some of which supported vases of fine porcelain, or jade figurines. Wall cabinets contained a collection of china and glassware. some of which, Miranda felt sure, dated back hundreds of years. It was a room which she felt instinctively even Lucy would not be allowed to enter. It would be all too easy for a careless toe to stumble over one of the richly coloured Bokhara rugs and send a fragile table flying, and with it, its priceless ornaments. It was also a room which served to deepen the gulf which Miranda already felt stretched between herself and the Cueras family.

She hesitated in the wide doorway, waiting for someone to notice her. Doña Isabella was there, talking to a tall man wearing the black robes of a priest who for a moment Miranda imagined to be Father Esteban. But when he turned to speak to Carla she saw that he was much younger than the elderly keeper of the monastery. Both Carla and Constancia were dressed alike this evening in long white gowns splashed with a floral design, and Miranda hoped she would have no difficulty in identifying them. She did not expect to do so; Carla's face was infinitely sharper than her sister's. Juan, his dark evening clothes suiting him very well, was talking to Constancia, and the third man with his back to her was unmistakably Rafael. But before anyone else observed her, Juan looked up and saw her standing there. With a brief word to Constancia he strode across the room to her side.

"Señorita!" he exclaimed, his eyes alight with admiration. "You—you look beautiful!"

Miranda forced a smile. "Don't sound so surprised," she teased, and he took her hand and raised it almost to his lips.

"No. I mean it." He shook his head. "I compliment you, *señorita.*"

Their conversation had attracted the attention of the other members of the group and after only a moment's hesitation Doña Isabella brought her companion across to be introduced.

"Father Domenico takes good care of our chapel in the valley, Miss Lord," she explained, after they had shaken hands. "He also lives at the monastery with Father Esteban."

Father Domenico's smile was warm. He was an attractive man, in his early forties, Miranda guessed, and he had not lost his appreciation of beauty during the course of his ascetic pursuits. "So you are the aunt of our little *niña, señorita?*" he queried. *"Qué es impossible!* You are so young!"

Miranda parried their compliments with a smile, always conscious that standing silently in the background was the man she most wanted to admire her. A fleeting glimpse had assured her that it was Rafael, lean and disturbingly attractive in evening clothes. He held a glass of some amber liquid in his hand and from the amount of attention it was receiving she thought he must find it absolutely fascinating. His behaviour irritated her. He had spoken more to her than any of the others. Why couldn't he be like Juan, like Father Domenico even? Why couldn't he greet her in the same friendly way as the rest of his family? But that wasn't entirely true, she admitted reluctantly. Carla still stood by the ornamental fireplace, her expression mirroring again that she was in no way enamoured of their unwelcome guest.

Miranda was provided with a drink and conversation became general. For her benefit they spoke in English, and only occasionally did Juan lapse into his native tongue. They dined by candlelight, and Miranda would have been enchanted had the reasons for her being there not troubled her so much. Silver candelabra shadowed centrepieces of interleaved magnolia and hibiscus blossoms, while the exquisite white lace mats were a fitting backcloth to finely wrought silver and crystal.

To Miranda's surprise, Rafael sat at the opposite end of the table from his mother, not Juan as she would have expected, with the twins on either side of him. Miranda sat at the other end of the table, near his mother, beside Father Domenico and opposite Juan.

The meal was slow and prolonged. Miranda found herself drinking rather a lot of wine, but it was something to do during the long discussions the men were having concerning the merits of various agricultural schemes. The women seemed quite content not to play a great part in the conversation, and although Miranda tried to speak to Doña Isabella about Lucy, the older woman seemed disinclined to listen while her sons were speaking. Or perhaps *sons* was the wrong denotation; it was Rafael who captured his mother's attention to the exclusion of everyone else.

85

Miranda was puzzled. Rafael's position in the household puzzled her. Previously, it had seemed quite a simple situation—the elder son inheriting the estate, the younger son dedicating his life to the sick. But was Rafael the younger son? He certainly looked younger than Juan, but perhaps the fact that Juan was so much stockier, so much swarthier, added to his years. And if he was not the younger son, why was Juan running the estate?

So many questions, so many perplexities; and not least of these her own confusion towards Juan's intentions with Lucy . . .

Coffee was served in the *sala*, and Juan adjusted some records on a turntable so that soon soft music of the guitar filled the room. Then he made, his way towards Miranda, standing with Constancia, admiring a jewelled silver crucifix from one of the wall cabinets.

"It is very old, *señorita*," he murmured in her ear, so that Miranda started, her fingers tightening for a moment over the carved stem.

"I have been telling Señorita Lord that this particular piece is reputed to have been brought to Guadalima by our ancestor, Alberto Cueras, Juan," explained Constancia, taking the crucifix again as Miranda held it out to her and putting it almost reverently back into its place.

"Our ancestor, *si*," Juan smiled. "And did Constancia also tell is more old than—er—*anos trecientos*?"

Miranda nodded. "It's quite beautiful. But then all religious relics have a certain mystique, don't they? I suppose they are imbued with the divine revelation of faith. What was it Tennyson wrote—*an arm clothed in white samite, mystic, wonderful*."

"And do you believe in mysticism, *señorita*?" enquired Father Domenico, suddenly appearing beside her.

"That rather depends on the connection, *señor*," replied Miranda carefully. "I believe in a divine presence. Whether or not that presence has manifested itself on earth is a matter for individual belief."

Father Domenico smiled. *"Muy discreto, señorita,* very discreet. You do not commit yourself. But you are not of the Faith, are you?"

"The Catholic faith, *señor*? No. But I keep an open mind."

"What is this?" Father Domenico frowned.

Miranda shrugged. "It means—the denomination of faith is less important to me than the faith itself."

Father Domenico was impressed. "That is an interesting theory, Miss Lord. I should like to discuss it with you further at some other time. I had not thought to find so mature an understanding on such young shoulders."

"Miss Lord is an interesting young woman, *padre*," remarked Rafael, but his tone indicated the irony with which he said the words.

Miranda, who had been unaware of him crossing the room to join them, felt her nerves tauten at his nearness, but Father Domenico turned to him eagerly and said:

"You agree, Rafael? It is an interesting conception, is it not? Something towards which the Ecumenical Council is constantly striving."

"And something with which you cannot agree, *padre*," commented Rafael dryly. "Can you?"

Father Domenico shrugged. "One does not need to catch a fish to enjoy the occupation of casting one's line, Rafael."

"And is that what you are doing, *padre*? Casting a line?"

The smile Father Domenico shared with Rafael was at once affectionate and challenging. "You know me too well, Rafael," he observed without rancour. "But I detect more than a little interest in your tones, too, my son."

Rafael shook his head. His hands were thrust deeply

into the pockets of his trousers and he seldom looked up from his apparent contemplation of the toes of his black suede boots.

Across the room, Doña Isabella was seated on a low striped sofa, dispensing coffee from a silver service. She chose that moment to beckon both her sons and Father Domenico towards her, and with reluctance Juan and the priest excused themselves to go and accept their cups. Constancia had already wandered off to examine the records by the player, and for the moment Miranda and Rafael were alone.

Although this was a situation which Miranda had desired above all things, now that it had happened she was at a loss. Unable to think of anything else, she murmured foolishly: "Oughtn't you to join your mother, too?"

Rafael glanced sideways at her, his gaze flickering over the creamy skin of her throat. "I am not a schoolboy, *señorita*. I am capable of making my own decisions."

Miranda flushed. "Oh, all right. I'm sorry I *presumed* to make a suggestion!"

Rafael studied her with intent dark eyes and she half wished he would resume his scrutiny of his boots. "It seems you have the knack of attracting both my brother and Father Domenico, *señorita*. That should compensate you for my lack of—deference."

Miranda's eyes mirrored the hurt he was deliberately inflicting. "Why do you say such things?" she exclaimed indignantly. Then she looked down at her hands. "Why don't you go and join your mother? It seems I don't attract you at least."

There was a moment's silence and then Rafael sighed. "All right, all right. I am sorry." He paused. "Tell me, how are you getting along with Lucy?"

Miranda looked up at him through her lashes. "I'm not."

"Qué?"

She shook her head. "I'm not getting on with her. I don't think I ever shall. Not here, anyway."

"Por qué?"

Miranda made a dismissing movement of her shoulders. "Your brother doesn't make it easy."

"No. No, he would not" Rafael expelled his breath through his nostrils. "Have you talked with the child?"

"Alone? No."

Rafael withdrew a hand from his pocket and ran it round the back of his neck, over the thick vitality of his hair. The gesture drew Miranda's attention to the muscles of his shoulders rippling easily beneath the fine cloth of his jacket. She wondered what he would do if she stretched out her fingers and touched the fine lace which ran down the front of his dress shirt. She knew what his skin was like beneath the silk—it was smooth and brown and covered with fine dark hair—

"—away from the hacienda."

Miranda came out of her daydream to find Rafael staring at her with impatient eyes.

"Did you hear what I said?" he demanded curtly, and when she shook her head apologetically, he stifled an expletive and went on: "I was saying that it would be better if you could talk to Lucy without my brother's presence. But not here. Away from the hacienda."

Miranda nodded. "And how do you propose I achieve that?" she enquired dryly. "Your brother will never permit me to take her anywhere—not alone at any rate."

Rafael scowled. "No. I don't suppose he would at that. Unless . . ." He paused. "Unless I take you both."

His offer was reluctant, she could sense it, and she didn't want to feel beholden to someone to whom her presence aroused distaste.

"It's quite all right. I'll think of something," she declined in a tight, polite little voice.

Rafael sighed. "Now what is wrong?"

"Well! You don't really want to take *me* anywhere, do you?"

He thrust his hand back into his pocket. "I would be prepared to do this."

"Oh, big deal!" Miranda was angry now. "Well, I can do without your assistance, thank you!"

"Rafael!" Doña Isabella's cultured tones broke into their exchange with cool inquiry. Neither of them had been aware of her approach and there was frowning speculation in the gaze she cast upon both of them. "Rafael, what is going on?"

Rafael half turned towards his mother. "I am sorry, Madrecita. You were wanting me, were you not?"

"I asked you what is going on, Rafael," insisted Doña Isabella, looking coldly at Miranda. "You seemed to be—arguing."

Rafael withdrew his hands from his pockets and buttoned his jacket. Then he linked his hands behind his back. "You are mistaken, Madrecita. Miss Lord and I were not—arguing, *Al contrario,* we were discussing the possibility of my taking Miss Lord and her niece to see the lake."

Miranda caught her breath, but Doña Isabella did not notice her surprise. She was too obviously surprised herself. "You, Rafael?" she queried doubtfully.

"*Si,* Madrecita. I am sure Juan will be glad to be relieved of his responsibilities for one morning, *no*?"

"I don't think—" Miranda was beginning indignantly, when he interrupted her.

"Miss Lord does not think my brother will object, Madrecita," he insisted, and short of contradicting him there and then Miranda had no choice but to remain silent.

Besides, deep inside her, a churning anticipation was weakening her resistance, turning her lower limbs to water. The prospect of a morning spent at some lake in

90

Rafael's company was as exciting as being able to talk to Lucy away from the overriding influence of the family. It was strange, she thought, how she seldom regarded Rafael as a member of the family.

Juan, however, was a different proposition. When he was told of the proposed expedition by his mother he immediately suggested that they all went. "We could—how you say?—picnic *no*?"

"No," said Rafael with quiet authority.

"*Por qué?*" Juan was sulky. "Is good idea!"

"Are there not jobs about the estate requiring your attention, *mi hermano*?" enquired Rafael coldly. "I hesitate to condemn your affection for the child, but are you not neglecting the affairs of the hacienda?"

Juan's plump face was flushed now. "You are not in a position to talk, Rafael!" he declared resentfully, but Rafael was not intimidated.

"*No obstante*, Juan. Miss Lord and myself will take the child alone. It is agreed?"

"When?" Juan was truculent.

"I am not certain." Rafael shrugged his shoulders. "Not tomorrow, *por lo menos*. Perhaps the next day, *si*?"

Miranda hid her disappointment. She should have known that Rafael would not be free the following day. And one more day would soon pass.

The party split up soon after this and Miranda did not have another opportunity of speaking to Rafael before he had Father Domenico departed together. Doña Isabella and Constancia went to see them off, while Juan helped himself to a liberal amount of cognac from the decanter on the side table. He was clearly put out after this unexpected turn of events and she hoped he would not do anything to make matters more difficult.

She was hesitating over whether or not to go on up to her room when Carla approached her. Miranda didn't want to speak to the other girl, but as Juan was there, albeit out of earshot, she could hardly ignore her and walk away.

"Well *señorita*," he commented Carla mockingly. "So you have decided to change your tactics, *no*?"

Miranda looked away. "I'd really rather not discuss it, *señorita*, if you don't mind."

"Oh, but I insist." Carla uttered a short laugh. "I find it most amusing. But you are wasting your time with Rafael. He cannot help you."

"I think I shall go to bed, *señorita*." Miranda would have walked away then, but Carla's hand on her arm detained her.

"*Momento, señorita*. A word of advice, if you like. Make Juan the object of your futile assault if you will, but leave Rafael alone. He is not attracted by your so obvious charms!" A malicious smile curved her lips. "He is not attracted by any woman, *señorita!*"

CHAPTER SIX

MIRANDA slept that night, although she had not expected to do so. Carla's parting words had disturbed her as the other girl had known they would, and she pondered them all the while she was taking off her clothes, showering her heated body, sliding between the silk sheets. But fortunately once her head touched the pillow oblivion came to claim her and she didn't awake until the sound of Lucy's shrill voice in the garden below her balcony made her aware that the sun was already high in the heavens.

Blinking, she struggled into a sitting position and then saw the untouched tray on her bedside table. The maid, Iñez, must have brought it earlier, but perhaps had been given instructions not to disturb her.

Frowning, she swung her legs out of bed and laid a hand beside the coffee pot. It was still quite warm and with a shrug she rose to her feet and taking up a silk robe walked to the windows. When she stepped on to the balcony, she could see that Lucy was not alone in the garden. One of the twins was with her, although Miranda couldn't be sure which one. She hesitated only a moment before shouting a greeting, and relaxed as Constancia's gentle face was turned up to hers.

"Hey, lazybones!" she called. "Do you know it is after ten o'clock?"

Miranda smiled. "I do now. If you give me a few moments to dress I'll come and join you." She switched her attention to the little girl, who was listening to their interchange silently. "Hello, Lucy. How are you this morning?"

Lucy shrugged indifferently. She was wearing another of the cotton dresses which Constancia had told Miranda had been made especially for her by Doña Isabella's seamstress. She thrust her hands into the deep patch pockets and kicked aimlessly at the ball with which she and Constancia had been playing.

"*Basta*, Lucy! Say good morning to the *señorita*!"

Miranda's lips tightened as Lucy glanced indifferently up at her and said: "Good morning, *señorita*."

It was useless remonstrating with her, trying to persuade her to say Aunt Miranda, or even just Miranda. Even Constancia persisted in the formal mode of address.

Leaving the balcony, Miranda went into the bathroom and in a matter of a few minutes she had washed and cleaned her teeth, and tugged a brush through her tumbled hair. She poured herself a cup of lukewarm coffee as she dressed in a sleeveless white sweater and navy blue jeans, and ate one of the *croissants* also provided before leaving her room.

However, when she reached the bottom of the stairs she encountered Juan coming out of the room to the left of the hall where he had been on the night of her arrival.

"Ah, Miss Lord!" he exclaimed, and his ill humour of the night before might never have been. "May I see you for a *momento*?".

Miranda's relief at his change of heart was short-lived when she nodded and he invited her into his study. She had not seen this room before and looked about her with interest as he indicated she should sit opposite him at his desk.

"Now, *señorita*," he murmured, flicking through some papers on his desk. "I have—how you say?—a *favor* to ask of you." He pointed to the wire trays on the desk which were overflowing with unanswered mail.

"*Oiga!* I am—most late with my replies, *si*? Father Esteban, he tells me you work as *secretario* in England, *no*?"

Miranda hands were clasped tightly together in her lap below the level of his gaze. "That's right, *señor*. I'm secretary to a merchant banker."

"Ah, so," Juan looked well pleased. He leaned back in his chair, making a pyramid of his fingers. "*Conque*, perhaps you will help me, *no*?"

"Help you, *señor*?"

"*Si*. As you see, there is much letters to write."

"You want me to write your letters for you, *señor*?" Miranda was not being deliberately obtuse, but his request had taken her by surprise.

"I wish you to—type my letters, *señorita*. *Por favor*. Is too much to ask?"

Miranda bent her head. It wasn't, of course. She was accepting his hospitality here and it was only right that she should try to repay that hospitality in any way she could. But he must know that by confining her to his study he was destroying any opportunity she might have had to spend the time with Lucy.

She looked up impatiently. Of course! That was why he was asking her this. It was his way of attempting to negate Rafael's offer of the night before. And she had thought he had forgotten that!

"When do you want me to do these letters, *señor*?" she asked formally.

Juan's eyes narrowed. Perhaps he was surprised that she had acquiesced so easily. "I—er—why—now, *señorita*?"

Miranda held up her head. "If it's all the same to you, *señor*, I'd prefer to work in the evenings. I do nothing in the evenings anyway, so—"

Juan's lips thinned. "I do not think so, *señorita*."

"Why not?" Miranda was prepared to argue for her rights.

"Is not suitable, *señorita*. He attempted a different

95

approach. "Come, *señorita*. They not take long, *no*?"

"You have prepared your replies?" Miranda was cool.

Juan shrugged. "We do—*dictato, si*?"

Miranda guessed he meant dictation and hid her irritation. After all, this was only one morning, and tomorrow . . . tomorrow . . .

But the tomorrow Miranda had envisaged did not take place. Much to her dismay, when she awoke the next morning, she found it was raining. And not just the steady drizzle she was used to back home. This was a torrential downpour, falling in a heavy curtain of water from a leaden sky. Lightning flicked from the mountain peaks and the rumble of thunder was a terrifying assault on her ears. Pools of mud appeared in the courtyard, and although the fountain was turned off it overflowed its stone basin. From the upper windows, it was possible to see the raging torrent which was the river; swollen with the waters running down from the mountains, it swirled dangerously on its way, and there was talk of the emergency measures which might have to be taken if it rose any higher up its banks. Valdez, the estate manager, came up to the hacienda for urgent discussions with Juan, and there was an air of suppressed excitement about the place.

No one had mentioned Rafael, it was obvious he would not come to take them out in this downpour, but Miranda wondered where he might be. Was he safe and dry in his stone house or was he, more likely, engaged in helping the villagers to protect what few possessions they had? She had plenty of time to indulge her imagination in this direction, for no one had the time to go and fetch Lucy, and as Juan was too busy to find jobs for her to do, Miranda spent the morning in her room. She sat by the balcony, watching the incredible demonstration of natural energy that was being enacted before her, and although she found this unexpected phenomenon fascinating, she couldn't help but feel anxiety at the fact that she had been in Guadalima almost a week and was no further forward in her plans for Lucy.

But what were her plans? What could she do? What *was* she going to do? Take the child away by force if necessary? She had that right, and yet—did she? The conversation she had had with Rafael on the way here troubled her continually. His implication had been that Juan had other plans for the child, and certainly Juan himself had reiterated that opinion by his actions. And Lucy was happy with Juan, that could not be denied, but how long would that happiness last if Juan grew bored with her, if he married and had children of his own? Rafael had said he was betrothed, that old-fashioned expression for being engaged, and although as yet she had seen no sign of his fiancée that fact could not be overlooked.

She stared unhappily at the rain streaming off the roof. Oh, if only it had been a fine day! If only she could have had Lucy to herself for a while, she might have been able to decide with more authority what was best for her. If it was fine tomorrow, would Rafael come then?

By late afternoon the rain had eased and the immediate fears of an emergency were relieved, and by dinner time it had ceased altogether. When Miranda stepped on to the floodlit terrace before going in for dinner the fragrance of the garden intoxicated her senses. The rain had driven away the faintly musky odour of putrescence that sometimes drifted up from the river, and everywhere felt fresh and invigorated. She was still standing there, a slim figure in her short-skirted apricot tunic, her palms warming the cooling flesh of her upper arms, when she saw headlights coming up the valley towards the hacienda.

Her immediate reaction was to turn and go into the

house, but the suspicion that it might be Rafael forced her to remain where she was. A few moments later the mud-splashed Landrover churned its way into the courtyard, and sure enough, Rafael himself swung down from the cabin. A grubby khaki shirt was plastered to his shoulders, jeans, also covered in mud, were pushed into rubber boots, and his hair was artificially darkened in its damp state. When he saw Miranda, a wry expression crossed his face, and he indicated his appearance expressively.

"I am not staying, *señorita*," he told her, one foot raised to rest on the shallow steps leading up to where she was standing. "It is you I came to see. As today was—how shall I say—washed out, *si*?—would tomorrow be suitable to you?"

Miranda licked dry lips. "To—to go to the lake with Lucy?"

"Where else?"

She shook her head. "That would be fine. Thank you."

Rafael nodded and would have turned away when she said: "You're soaked to the skin! What have you been doing?"

He looked back at her. "It has been raining, *señorita*, or have you not noticed?"

Miranda sighed. "I know. But—well, how did you get so wet?"

Rafael dug the toe of his boot into the mud. "One of my brother's labourers was swept into the river, *señorita*. Fortunately, we were able to get a rope to him and haul him out. Unfortunately, one of his rescuers was not so lucky."

"You mean—someone has been drowned?" Miranda was distressed.

"Did Juan not tell you?" Rafael shook his head. "No, perhaps he would not. However, that is the way of things, is it not? And now—" He looked down at his dishevelled appearance. "Now, I must go and get dry."

"You need a hot bath," exclaimed Miranda impulsively. "Why don't you have one here? I am sure Juan has some clothes you could borrow—"

Her voice trailed away as she realised what she was saying, how casually she was using his brother's Christian name, but Rafael was swinging himself back into the Landrover. "I do have hot water at my house, *señorita*," he commented curtly, and without another word drove away.

As Miranda entered the wide hall of the hacienda she encountered Constancia, who looked beyond the English girl expectantly. "Was that not the Landrover, *señorita*?" she exclaimed.

Miranda tossed a strand of hair over her shoulder. "As a matter of fact, yes."

Constancia withdrew her gaze from some point beyond the terrace and focussed on the other girl's face. "It was Rafael?" she asked in surprise.

"Yes." Miranda felt more and more uncomfortable under that penetrating stare. "He—he didn't stop. He just came—to tell me that—that he'll take Lucy and me to the lake tomorrow."

"I see." Constancia looked impatient. "Was that all he said, *señorita*?"

Not knowing whether or not she ought to tell the other girl about the drowned man, Miranda nodded. "I'm— I'm afraid so. He—he was soaked. I expect he's gone home to get dry."

"This is my brother's home, *señorita*," declared Constancia, with a little of her mother's hauteur, and Miranda hoped she was not going to behave as unsociably towards her as did her sister.

Over dinner, Constancia informed the rest of the family that Rafael had called and spoken to Miranda. They all seemed surprised that he had visited the hacienda without making his presence generally known, and

Doña Isabella looked positively distressed. Miranda was left with the feeling that they all thought she had been responsible for his abrupt departure. She was glad when the meal was over and she could seek the solitude of her own room. Beautiful though the hacienda might be, she was not happy in its imposing surroundings.

The following morning dawned with a golden heat haze clouding the sun. It was one of those delightful mornings that sometimes follows a storm, when everything appears especially brilliant, greener, brimming with vitality. Miranda, who had not slept very well, was up and dressed in a cream cotton shirt and cream pants by six-fifteen, and on impulse made her way downstairs to the kitchen in the hope of making an early breakfast.

Jezebel was already about, chivvying the other servants, supervising their chores and generally making her presence felt. She stared at the English girl in surprise when Miranda tentatively put her head around the kitchen door, and then demanded to know what she wanted at this hour.

Miranda opened the door wider and entered the large, well-lit kitchen, with its lines of polished units, its mechanised equipment, and long scrubbed table. Pale blue and lemon rubber tiles were soft underfoot, and a coffee percolator bubbled aromatically on a split-level stove. A door stood wide to the back of the house, and she could hear the sound of goatbells in the distance.

"I—well, I was wondering whether I might trouble you for some coffee," Miranda admitted nervously. For all her age and dimunitive stature, Jezebel was an intimidating personality.

"*Asi!* You wish coffee here, *señorita?*"

Miranda shrugged. "Anywhere—if you don't mind."

Jezebel glanced at the startled Indian boy who was hovering near the oven with a tray of curled *croissants* for baking, and snapped him into action with a rapid command in his own language. Then she looked back at Miranda and to Miranda's surprise her expression softened.

"You will sit?" she offered, indicating the long form which flanked the table, and Miranda nodded and seated herself. "Is today you go to lake with Don Rafael," Jezebel went on, taking cups from shelves, setting a small try with cream jug and sugar basin. "Is it not, *señorita . . .*"

"Why, yes." Miranda tipped her head on one side. "But how do you know that? We were supposed to go yesterday."

Jezebel smiled then, revealing only a few stumps of teeth "Jezebel hear you talking to Don Rafael last evening, *señorita*," she said, tapping significantly at her ear. Then she frowned. "The *señorita* likes Don Rafael, *no*?"

Miranda was taken aback and she rested her elbows on the table, cupping her chin in her hands to hide her reddening cheeks. "Don Rafael—has been very kind. He has offered to take me and—"

"—the *niña*. Yes, yes, I know, *señorita*." Jezebel poured coffee into an almost transparent china cup. "*Alli*, is good, *si*?"

Miranda accepted the coffee gratefully. "Very good. Thank you, Jezebel."

The affairs of the kitchen distracted the old housekeeper for a few minutes and Miranda was relieved. Much as she appreciated the old woman's good humour, she didn't want to get involved in a discussion of the merits of the various members of the Cueras family.

Before Jezebel was free again, however, the door suddenly opened and Rafael himself walked in, his brows lifting interrogatively at the sight of Miranda.

"*Buenos dias, señorita!*" he greeted her gravely, and then a smile lifted the corners of his mouth as he saw Jezebel. "*Como esta, vieja!*"

They spoke together in their own language and

Miranda would have given a lot to know exactly what they were saying. That she figured in their exchange was obvious from the gestures Jezebel was making, but she also noticed that Rafael avoided certain questions, shaking his head goodhumouredly. After a few minutes, he put Jezebel aside and went to help himself to coffee. After the first mouthful, he coughed, and making a brief apology he walked to the table and looked down at Miranda.

"*Bien, señorita,* what is it they say? Could you not sleep?"

Miranda moved her shoulders indifferently. "I was awake. I—I did think we might be leaving quite early."

"How astute!" He quirked one eyebrow.

Miranda was glad of her cup between her fingers to disguise her nervousness. "How are you this morning *señor?*"

Rafael drank some more coffee, and frowned impatiently as he relapsed into a spate of coughing again. "I appear to have developed a slight congestion, *señorita.* But it is not serious. It will pass."

"I'm not surprised," exclaimed Miranda, shocked by her own temerity. "Wearing wet clothes!"

Rafael studied her indignant face for a disruptive moment, then he turned away. "Yes—well, you might be right, *señorita*," he agreed dryly. "But one cannot always leave a man to drown simply because one wishes to change into dry clothes!"

"But you were still wearing them when you came up here last night," she protested, to his broad, denim-clad back.

Rafael glanced round at her. "Someone had to tell the man's wife that her husband was dead, *señorita*," he stated expressionlessly. "She lives not too far from here." He turned away again. "Ah—Jezebel, are those *croissants* ready? May I have one?"

Miranda stared mutinously down at the wooden table.

She felt suitably chastened. But she hadn't know that he had been breaking such news when he came up to the hacienda. Although she did recall his withdrawal, his refusal to enter the building.

Jezebel set a basket of hot *croissants* in the middle of the table, put out a dish of yellow butter, a jar of conserve. *"Siéntese, señor,"* she insisted, almost pushing him into the seat. "You and the *señorita* may share a meal, *si?*"

Rafael shrugged, his eyes flickering over Miranda only fleetingly. *"A fondo, Jezebel. Gracias!"*

Miranda couldn't enjoy the intimacy of the situation because of what had gone before, and also because Jezebel hovered in the background like a predatory black crow. As soon as Rafael's coffee cup was empty she swooped to refill it, watching him eating with evident satisfaction.

"Es bien, señor?" she asked eagerly, and he smiled and said: *"Excelente, Jezebel, como usual. Muy gracias."*

When the meal was over, Rafael rose to his feet, finishing the dregs of his coffee as he did so. "You are ready, *señorita?*"

Miranda nodded and rose too. "Of course."

"Bien. We will collect the *niña* on our way."

Miranda glanced at her watch. It was only a little after seven. Surely too early for any member of the household to be about.

"I—I ought to leave a message," she faltered.

"Jezebel will tell my mother where you have gone, *señorita*. Come! We will have the better part of the day, *si?*"

Driving away from the hacienda, Miranda felt an overpowering feeling of excitement. Jezebel had come to the terrace to wave them off and there was about her expression a certain suppressed satisfaction at this turn of events. Miranda couldn't understand it—unless it had something to do with what Carla had said—something about Rafael not being interested in women. But that couldn't be true. He wasn't *that* kind of a man, she would stake her life on it. And besides, sometimes—only sometimes—when he looked at her, she had seen a certain reluctant awareness in his eyes . . .

She thrust such thoughts aside. She was not here to indulge in fantasies about herself and Rafael. She was to have at least half a day with Lucy and somehow she had to get through to her.

The fields in the valley were still running with water from the storm, but the people working barefoot in their midst still stopped to wave as they passed.

"Are the crops ruined?" exclaimed Miranda, concern dispelling the tension she had felt earlier.

Rafael glanced out of his window and made a slight movement of his shoulders. "Some will be, some will not. It is—as they say—the will of God. These people are happy to be alive." His tone was indulgent as he turned to look at her. "Do you not agree that this is the important thing, *señorita*?"

Miranda stared steadily at him for a few moments, but then she had to look away. "I—suppose so."

"You would not agree? Of course not. You are from that materialistic society where a man is judged on the property he possesses."

"That's not entirely true—"

"No?" Rafael's jaw hardened. "It is the same every-where, *señorita*. I am not condemning your society any more than my own. And indeed, there are points on both sides. For all I accept that a man's life—the *quality* of a man's life—is the important thing, there are times when I find my beliefs stretched to a degree. Babies are born; they die; who can honestly say that such a futile existence merits a place in the scheme of things?"

"You mean—because of the—conditions . . ."

"Conditions are worse in other places, *señorita*. At

104

least my country is not torn apart by civil war, at least a man can be sure—or reasonably sure, at least—of reaching his middle years."

Miranda was fascinated. "Is that why you're a doctor, *señor*? Instead of the *patron*?"

Rafael's expression hardened. "We were not talking about me, *señorita*. Perhaps you should be occupying your time by considering the approach you intend to make to your niece. I warn you—my brother can be a formidable adversary."

Miranda flushed. "I have already discovered what kind of an adversary your brother is, *señor*."

Rafael frowned. "What do you mean?"

Miranda shook her head. "It's not important."

"Please—I want to know."

Rafael was very persuasive. Miranda couldn't help the tingle that ran along her veins at the thought of how persuasive he would be if he was saying: *"Please—I want to make love to you."*

"Señorita!"

His harsh command brought her to her senses. "I—well—oh, he had me helping him, *señor*. Typing his letters, filing his correspondence!"

Rafael scowled. "When?"

"A couple of days ago." Miranda was uncomfortable. "I owe it to him, after all. He is permitting me to stay at the hacienda—"

The word Rafael uttered under his breath would have been understandable in any language, and his mouth was clamped tightly together. "You will do no further secretarial work for my brother, *señorita*," he stated bleakly. "I will see to that."

Miranda didn't know what to reply. "Thank you," she murmured awkwardly.

When the Landrover turned into the overgrown courtyard of the monastery, Lucy herself came scampering out of the building to see who was there. When she saw Miranda and Rafael, however, her face visibly drooped and she fell back a pace.

"Hello, Lucy," said Miranda, getting out of the Land-rover and walking towards her smilingly. "Er—Don—Don Rafael and I have come to take you for a ride."

Lucy's lips curled. "I don't want to go for a ride in that dirty old thing!" she exclaimed scornfully. "Tio Juan will be coming to take me out in his car."

"No, he will not, Lucy," returned Rafael, ignoring her rudeness. "Now, where is the *padre*?"

"*Heme aqui,*" called Father Esteban from the doorway of the building. "Please—you come in? I can offer you some milk, *si*?"

"Goat's milk?" Rafael raised his eyebrows questioningly at Miranda and she made a helpless gesture. "*A fondo, padre*. We will come in for five minutes, *no*?"

Father Esteban led the way along a cold stone corridor to where he and Lucy had been sharing a simple meal. There was milk and cornbread and a dish of oranges and peaches. The room was stone-walled and chill after the heat of the day, but neither Father Esteban nor Lucy seemed to notice.

Rafael indicated that Miranda should be seated in the chair beside the plain table, while he lounged on a stool against the wall. Lucy, who had followed them inside reluctantly, hovered in the doorway, her lips moving rebelliously.

The goat's milk was a lighter texture than ordinary milk, Miranda found, and although she was not a great lover of milk of any kind, it was not unpalatable. She refused anything to eat and listened while Rafael and the priest spoke together. They mostly used their native tongue, for Father Esteban was clearly happier in that, but later he announced that Lucy was teaching him English and that soon he expected to be properly proficient. Lucy responded to his gentle teasing, clearly feeling a great affection for him, too, but when the time

106

came for them to leave she refused to let go of his hand.

"I want to stay with you, Father," she cried urgently. "Don't make me go away. Tio Juan is coming."

Father Esteban shook his head. "Not today, *niña*, not today. Come, your aunt is here to see you only."

Lucy sniffed pathetically. "She's not my aunt. Tio Juan says I am a little Mexican girl now, and she is English!"

Rafael exchanged a glance with Miranda and she was warmed by the compassion she saw in his eyes. "Tio Juan should not say such things to you, Lucy," he declared quietly. "You are English. Why else do you speak that language? And—and your aunt is very hurt when you speak so unkindly to her. You must remember, she has known you since you were a very little girl—a baby, in fact. And she also remembers your mother and father. Your mother was her sister. How do you think she feels, knowing that you are denying your own family? Do you think Tio Juan would deny his own family? Because I do not."

"But Tio Juan told me that she wants to take me back to England with her, and England is a cold country where the sun never shines."

Rafael made an impatient gesture. "Tio Juan has never been to England. He does not know what it is like."

"Have *you*?" Lucy stared up at him appealingly.

"Of course." Rafael ignored the way Miranda's eyes widened.

"And does the sun shine there?" persisted Lucy.

"*Naturalmente*. Without the sun, we should all die, *pequeña*."

"But what is it like?"

Rafael hesitated. "It is a small country, but a green country. A country of many contrasts. But its people are very friendly, very kind."

Lucy's lips trembled. "But what if I don't like it?"

107

Rafael put a reassuring hand on her shoulder. "Lucia, nothing is decided yet, *no*? Let us face every consequence as it occurs. Come with us this morning, and perhaps, who knows, you may find your aunt is not the—how you say?—*ogre?*—you think her."

Lucy looked uncertainly at Miranda. "All right. All right, I'll come. But—but I want to sit in front. With you." She looked at Rafael once more.

"We will all sit in front, *pequeña*," essayed Rafael tolerantly. *"Adios, padre. Hasta luego!"*

As they all walked towards the Landrover, Miranda murmured in a low voice: "I didn't realise you'd been to England, *señor*."

Rafael looked penetratingly down at her. "I have not, *señorita*."

"But—" Miranda's lips parted in confusion.

"It was an acceptable deception, *no*?" Rafael's eyes challenged hers. "I will make my confession *de Neustra Señora*, I promise."

Miranda frowned. "What does that mean?"

Rafael shook his head and bent to lift Lucy into the front of the Landrover. "It is a matter between me and my conscience. *señorita*. Shall we go?"

CHAPTER SEVEN

RAFAEL drove away from the monastery following a winding track which hitherto Miranda had not noticed. It was little more than a goat track really and she doubted that any vehicle other than a Landrover could have made it. They drove up between stunted gorse and pine trees, steadily climbing away from the monastery until when she looked back the mission and the houses further down the valley looked doll-like and unreal. The underbrush gave way as they reached a narrow pass along a rocky precipice with a hair-raising drop on one side and the sheer wall of the mountain on the other. It was much cooler up here, too, and Miranda shivered when she thought of some cold grey stretch of water.

"Where are we going?" demanded Lucy at last, possibly becoming conscious of Miranda's taut body beside hers.

Rafael took a moment to glance at the child. "We are going to a lake, Lucia," he said calmly. "You know what a lake is, do you not?"

"Of course." Lucy was indignant. "But where is it? How can there be a lake in the mountains?"

"There are often lakes in the mountains," replied Miranda, forcing herself not to think of how easily it would be for the muddy track below them to cause the wheels of the Landrover to slide and pitch them all over the precipice. "Mountains create natural basins where water gathers. Particularly after rains like we had yesterday."

Rafael shook his head. "The lake we seek is not that kind of a lake, *señorita*. But you will see—very soon."

His enigmatic words had the effect of banishing

Miranda's nervousness, and she allowed the anticipation she had felt earlier to envelop her again. She was eager to reach their destination and even Lucy showed a growing curiosity.

The sheer walls of rock enclosed them for a space as they passed through its face, and then they emerged above a small canyon and Rafael stopped the Landrover so they could look down. At its base, Miranda could see the gleam of blue-green water, vaguely misty in the early morning light, while the lushly foliaged walls of the canyon were in marked contrast to the bare rock they had encountered so far.

"A natural phenomenon, is it not?" queried Rafael, with obvious appreciation of the two girls' amazement. "Can you see the steam rising from the water? There is a hot spring which feeds the lake. The water is always warm."

Miranda gasped. "It—it's beautiful!" she exclaimed. "But—do we go down?"

Rafael nodded, starting the vehicle's engine again. "For a short way. There is a plateau above the lake. We can climb down quite easily from there."

"But how do we get up again?" wailed Lucy, as the Landrover began the steep ascent.

"Do not be a mouse, Lucia," chided Rafael, the tautness of his tone belying the casualness of his words. "Is this not an adventure?"

"I don't like it here!" declared Lucy tremulously.

She was looking at the high mountains all about them with obvious unease, and her fingers plucked nervously at the material of her dress. Her agitation drew Miranda's attention from the excited observation of her surroundings and her brows drew together in a frown. Had this been Rafael's intention in bringing them here? Had he thought that Lucy might be frightened here— might be shocked into remembering some other canyon, some other mountain?

"I want to go back to the monastery," insisted Lucy, pushing her thumb into her mouth, a gesture which Miranda recognised with a pang. If there had been any lingering doubt in her mind that the child was Lucy, that gesture would have banished it. Susan expended more time and more angry words in trying to dissuade Lucy from sucking her thumb than any other habit she had developed.

"Don't be silly, Lucy," she said now, putting her arm round the little girl and in so doing accidentally brushing Rafael's shoulder with her fingers. He flinched from her touch and she quickly withdrew her arm and contented herself with taking Lucy's hands. "Darling, there's nothing to be afraid of. Raf—*Don* Rafael knows what he is doing. There's no danger."

"I just don't like it here," maintained Lucy tearfully. "It's so—so lonely."

"You are not alone, Lucia," said Rafael briefly, giving all his attention to bringing the Landrover to a halt on a small promontory overhanging the lake. "See! We are here! Are you not going to paddle in the shallows?"

Lucy looked at him uneasily. "Is—is it deep?" she asked, controlling her tears with evident difficulty.

Rafael swung down from the Landrover and leaning in lifted the child out, too. "Come!" he said. "I will show you, *si*? With me you will have no fear, *no*?"

When Rafael chose to exert the charm which as yet Miranda had only experienced directed towards his mother and sisters, no one, not even Lucy, could remain aloof. Below the jutting plateau of rock, a steeply sloping footway gave access to the shores of the small lake. It was slippery now after all the rain, but Rafael was clearly used to negotiating its uneven surface and he carried Lucy down confidently before coming back to help Miranda. He held out his hand to assist her, and Miranda put hers into it, but her feet gave way below her at the first step and she lost her balance and slithered

111

down the muddy incline to his feet.

If Rafael found the picture of her, mud-splashed and embarrassed, amusing, he hid it very well and advised her not to try and brush the mud away but wait until it dried when it would flake off very easily.

Down here in the canyon, it was much warmer, and the sun glinted on the water invitingly. Miranda wished she had had a bathing suit to bring with her, but she had not expected to need such garments. Instead, she walked with Lucy to the water's edge and marvelled at the tiny spring which shed its warmth into the pool. The unusual heat generated by the water was responsible for the luxuriant growth of flowers and trees, but Miranda couldn't help considering that in such tropical surroundings all manner of insect life would flourish, too.

Lucy's initial suspicion and uneasiness gave way to enthusiasm as she kicked off one small sandal and dipped a delicate toe into the water. "It is warm! It's really warm!" she exclaimed, and Miranda hid the disappointment which came from the realisation that that momentary awareness of something terrible which had happened to her had vanished once more into the inner regions of Lucy's mind.

Rafael brought a rubber sheet down from the Land-rover and spread it on the ground. Then he stretched his length upon it, clearly disposed to leave Miranda to deal with Lucy. But Lucy was more interested in exploring, and after an awkward look at Rafael, Miranda followed her on a partial circumnavigation of the lake. She tried to tell herself that every moment spent in Lucy's company was a moment nearer the truth, but she hadn't a lot of confidence in that supposition.

For a while Lucy was content to examine the purple and white orchids which grew on the trunks of the trees near the water's edge, exclaiming every now and then when some new specimen caught her eye. Lizards scuttled away at their approach, and once a long snake uncoiled itself and slid away into the tall grass. This latter encounter unnerved Miranda sufficiently to consider shouting to Rafael; but he had closed his eyes, and in any case, Lucy dismissed her fears nonchalantly by saying that Father Esteban had told her to be beware of the smaller, poisonous vipers and the more obvious rattlesnake. Overhead, birds kept up a constant chatter at this intrusion into their privacy, and had it not been for the more serious aspects of the situation Miranda would have been entranced herself.

As it was, she felt a vague resentment that having brought them here Rafael should so indifferently abandon his responsibility. And yet what could he say? It was up to her, Miranda, to make some effort, no matter how small. Brushing a careless hand over her hips and then uttering an irritated exclamation at the forgotten mud which came away on her fingers, she was encouraged by Lucy's giggles at her annoyance. Rubbing her hands together, she said quietly: "Don't you remember me at all, Lucy?"

Lucy glanced quickly away. "No."

Miranda sighed. "Are you sure?"

"Of course, I'm sure. Oh—look! Isn't that a beautiful butterfly! What do you think it's called?"

Miranda cast an impatient look at the butterfly. "I don't know. A red admiral or something," she answered uncaringly, mentioning the name of the first butterfly that came into her head. "Lucy, don't you want to remember?"

"It's not a red admiral," stated Lucy definitely. "They're much smaller and they have sort of black and white markings near the tops of their wings."

"I don't particularly care what a red admiral looks like," retorted Miranda. "Lucy, when we came down here, you remembered something, didn't you? Something that frightened you?" Then she halted abruptly. "How do you know what a red admiral looks like?"

Lucy raised her small eyebrows. "I don't know."

"Lucy, red admirals are not found in South America—in Mexico, that is—they're found in Europe. Doesn't that prove to you that what I'm telling you is the truth? How would you know about English butterflies unless you had lived in England—unless you were English?"

Lucy turned away. "I probably read about it somewhere," she said, shrugging her small shoulders.

"Oh, *Lucy*!"

Lucy glanced reluctantly round at her and Miranda could see her lips were trembling. "I don't know who I am, I truly don't. But even if I am who you say I am, I still want to stay with Tio Juan!" And she stumbled away kicking stones.

Miranda felt a wave of inadequacy sweep over her. It was too much for her. She simply couldn't handle this alone. She didn't know how. She had never had to deal with an amnesiac before. How could she be expected to know what to do—what to say? Anger rose in her throat, and because there was no one else to direct it against she left Lucy to her explorations and walked quickly back to where Rafael was lying. She stood looking down at him impatiently, unwillingly aware of the latent attraction he held for her. But as though he had become aware of her scrutiny his eyes flickered open.

With an exclamation in his own language, he sprang to his feet. *"Si, señorita?"*

Miranda's lips pursed angrily. "I want to ask you something, *señor*. Has anyone—any doctor, that is— seen the child?"

Rafael frowned. "But of course. Doctor Rodrigues—"

"I don't mean some general practitioner!" she exclaimed, interrupting him scornfully. "I'm talking about a specialist! Someone specialising in amnesia and allied disturbances."

114

"I do know what a specialist is, *señorita*," he remarked mildly, and she could feel her cheeks reddening in spite of herself. "And yes, my brother brought a Doctor Delgado out from Mexico City several weeks ago."

"And what was his diagnosis?"

Rafael moved his shoulders. "I gather he expressed the opinion that it is only a matter of time before she recovers her memory."

"You gather—" Miranda clenched her fists. "But you said you were a doctor! Didn't you discuss it with him?"

"Pardon me, *señorita*, I did not say I was a doctor."

"You said you were entitled to put M.D. after your name!" she declared indignantly.

"I am." Rafael spread his hands. "But I am no specialist, *señorita*."

Miranda shifted her weight from one foot to the other. "But you must have an opinion. I—I don't know what to do."

She could hear the break in her voice and turned angrily away. The very last thing she wanted to do was break down in front of him. Just because of what Lucy had said she must not begin to feel defeated. She was the child's guardian, not Juan Cueras.

"*Señorita*, as I said before, you do not give this time," he commented quietly.

"I don't have the time!" she retorted in a muffled voice.

"Then perhaps you should think again." Rafael sounded impatient now. "*Señorita*, you came here to find a child who for four months has lived in our valley—has shared our community life—has become accustomed to our ways. In one week—two weeks—you expect to change all this. I tell you, it is too soon, too quick! She cannot possibly be expected to accept such a drastic change of circumstances without protest. If she had recognised you, of course—"

"But she didn't, did she?" Tears stung Miranda's eyes as she turned back to him. "So what am I supposed to do? Take—I don't know—four months to convince her she is who I say she is? I *can't*. I don't have the time, or—or the money."

Rafael shrugged his broad shoulders. "I agree, it is a difficult situation."

"Difficult? *Difficult?*" Miranda could hear her voice rising, but she couldn't help it. "It's impossible! Every time I try to talk to her she seems to put up a mental block against me. I don't know what to say to her to win her confidence. Can't you help me? You have some experience. *Please!*"

Impulsively, she stretched out her hand and gripped his tanned forearm. His flesh was cool beneath her moist fingers and she had an urgent desire to move even closer to him as though by creating a physical intimacy she could arouse a mental affinity between them. He was so adept at remaining aloof, but right now she needed his sympathy.

But her momentary hopes were shattered when he wrenched his arm out of her grasp and stepped back away from her. "I can do nothing," he declared in a harsh voice, and when her eyes were drawn irresistibly to his taut face she was shocked by the expression in his dark eyes. She could almost believe he hated her, and her fragile hopes of his assistance splintered. She moved her head helplessly. She had known her company irritated him, but until now she had not realised how much.

"I—I'm sorry," she got out tremulously. "I—I should have known better than to appeal to any member of—of the Cueras family!"

A spasm of pain twisted his face. "Do not say that! It is not true. I would help you if I could, but I cannot."

Miranda's lips curled contemptuously. "Would you? Why? You obviously despise me. I can't imagine why unless you, as well as your brother, have some reason for wanting Lucy here."

"My feelings are not to do with your niece, *señorita*," stated Rafael coldly. "*Por dios*, why can you not accept that in my opinion you are rushing things? Stay awhile. I have told you my mother will accommodate you."

Miranda thrust her thumbs into the low belt of her jeans. "I do not enjoy staying at the hacienda," she declared unsteadily. "And in any case, I have to get back to England. Just because your sisters and your mother can afford to do nothing all their lives it does not mean that everyone shares that same position—or would want to. As a matter of fact, I—I enjoy my work. And I don't want to lose my job."

Rafael's fingers closed over the medallion which rested on his chest. "Then there is nothing more to be said."

"Isn't there?" Miranda looked at him angrily. "Do you honestly believe your brother will allow me to take Lucy without a struggle?"

"Father Esteban will see that my brother does what is best for the child, *señorita*," stated Rafael stiffly.

"How ambiguous! And what do you think he will decide? How can my modest apartment compare with the undoubted opulence of the hacienda? Father Esteban depends upon your brother's good will for his livelihood, doesn't he? We all have to live, *señor*."

"Do not be bitter, *señorita*. The situation will resolve itself. Situations always do."

"I wish I could believe that." Miranda stared unhappily across the lake to where Lucy was squatting on some rocks trailing her fingers in the water. "Oh, God I wish—I wish—"

She halted uncertainly. What did she wish? That she had never come here? That there had never been an accident? Oh, that, of course. But had there been no occasion for her to visit the valley of the Lima she would

117

never have met Rafael Cueras, and in spite of everything that was a circumstance she would not have avoided. But why? *Why?* He had no time for her—indeed, he despised her. And on those odd occasions when she had imagined she felt a certain awareness between them he had quickly dispelled it by his coldness and his rejection of anything approaching intimacy. What had Carla meant by that cruel statement that Rafael was not interested in women? It wasn't true—it couldn't be true . . .

She was so wrapped up in her own thoughts that she wasn't immediately aware that Rafael had left her until she heard the trill of Lucy's laughter across the water and saw Rafael squatting beside her, pointing at something they could both see beneath the surface. A pain tore at her stomach and she sank down on to the rubber groundsheet, legs crossed, chin resting on her knuckles. What was there about her that he disliked so much? she asked herself miserably. Why, when he could be so charming to his mother and sisters, so gentle with Lucy, so polite and considerate to the people of the valley, did he continually treat her like a leper? Even if the attraction was all on her side, and even if she did irritate him, surely he could at least be civil to her! She wondered what he was saying to Lucy now, what was causing the child's mouth to tremble with laughter, her cheeks to turn pink with enjoyment. Was he telling her that she had nothing to worry about? That her aunt wouldn't dream of taking her from the valley by force? And that even if she tried to do so, her two adopted uncles would be there to stop her?

Miranda looked down at her toes. She felt ashamed of her thoughts. She had no reason, no reason at all, to suppose that Rafael was playing a double game. On the contrary, he had gone out of his way to give her this time alone with the child. Just because she had made no good use of it was not his fault.

She looked up and saw that the others had left the lake and were climbing the rocks at the far side of the canyon, Rafael giving Lucy his hand to haul her up beside him. Miranda pressed her lips together, trying not to feel envious. He could not have made it more obvious that he did not desire her company and she could only hope that what he was saying to the child would in some way encourage her to have more faith in others beside Juan. But again, she had no part in it, and the immense sense of loneliness she felt was magnified a hundred times.

Getting to her feet, she walked along the lakeside, deliberately ignoring Rafael and Lucy. A rotten tree trunk was lying half into the water, its roots torn up and spongy with termite holes. No delicate orchids adorned its stem, even the parasitic plant life knew it was dead. Miranda kicked carelessly at the trunk getting a certain amount of relief from causing her pain. But when an enormous black beetle emerged and paused for a moment, seemingly looking at her, she couldn't suppress a shiver.

With a grimace she turned away and as she did so she saw floating out on the lake, half hidden by the rotten trunk of the tree, an enormous waterlily. The beetle had disappeared now and without hesitation she climbed on to the spongy trunk and walked carefully along its length. Squatting down, she reached for the blossom, but without warning her weight caused the trunk to shift slightly and she pitched forward into the lake.

She came up gasping, as much from unpleasant dragging sensation caused by her clothes as from actual shock. The water was warm, but she had never swum fully clothed before and the garments were clinging to her.

In those first few dramatic seconds she was only concerned with making the shallows and was completely unaware that Rafael had observed her plight until he surfaced beside her, shaking the water from his hair.

119

"Do not panic!" he exclaimed urgently. "I will help you."

"I—I can manage," protested Miranda, but he ignored her, supporting her head with one hand and swimming strongly back to the side. When they reached the shallows, he allowed her feet to touch the bottom for only a moment while he gained his feet and then he swung her up into his arms again and carried her up the pebbly shore to where he had laid the groundsheet. Miranda felt quite lightheaded at this unexpected turn of events and it was a temptation to pretend a terror she did not feel and put her arms around his neck.

However, a spasm of coughing caught him unawares and he had to put her down more quickly than she had expected. She stumbled and would have fallen had he not reached out and grasped her arm, but her weight threw them off balance and they fell together, the weight of his body almost knocking the breath out of her.

"Oh, perdone, señorita," he muttered automatically thrusting himself up with his hands behind her head, looking down into her startled green eyes.

"I—I'm all right," she managed, catching her breath. "You—you haven't hurt me."

Rafael moved his head slowly up and down, but the dark eyes did not move from her face. They lingered on the flushed curve of her cheek, the slanting darkness of her lashes, the parted softness of her mouth. Miranda felt a worse constriction than she had felt before and as he continued to let his body rest on hers she felt the hardening of his thighs and the spreading warmth of desire stirring between them. She wasn't mistaken this time, and a yielding lethargy entered her limbs.

"Rafael . . ." she breathed achingly, but with a frightening change of mood, Rafael's expression had hardened into angry disgust.

"Cristo!" he groaned, dragging himself up and away from her. *"Estoy loco rematado!"* His fists clenched by

120

his sides, water dripping unheeded from his shirt and pants. "Get up! Get up, *señorita*! We leave—at once!"

Lucy, who had watched what had occurred from the far side of the lake, now came running towards them, but her lips drooped disappointedly when she overheard Rafael's last words. "We're leaving, Tio Rafael?" she exclaimed in dismay. "But why? Why?" She looked down resentfully at Miranda. "Why can't she just take off her clothes and dry them in the sun? Why must we all go back just because she was stupid?"

Miranda scrambled indignantly to her feet. She had had just about enough. "It may have missed your notice, Lucy, but your—your—Don Rafael—is soaked, too!" She stumbled over the words.

"I know. Because he had to rescue you!" retorted Lucy.

"No one had to rescue me," replied Miranda bitterly. "I was perfectly capable of making the shallows myself." She glanced at Rafael and felt angry that he could so coldly dismiss that devastating moment which had left her feeling weak and hurt and oddly vulnerable. But at least she had proved one thing, she thought without enthusiasm. He was not indifferent to a woman, to the feel of a woman's body against his . . .

"Anyway," Lucy was going on, "Tio Rafael can take off his shirt, and his trousers will soon dry—"

"Your uncle needs to get into dry clothes," returned Miranda fiercely, realising that his wellbeing was none of her affair but unable to prevent herself anyway. "He already has a cold from the last time!"

"Well, you shouldn't have climbed on that silly old log!" declared Lucy scornfully. "I thought grown-ups were supposed to have more sense—"

"*Bastante*, Lucia!" Rafael silenced the little girl with a curt command. He was unbuttoning his shirt as he spoke and tugging it off his wet shoulders. Although his trousers still clung wetly to his hard body he seemed to have

121

himself in control again. "We will go, as I have said. *Immediatemente*. The *señorita*—your aunt—can take off her wet garments and wrap herself in the rug I keep in the Landrover. Myself, I will survive until we get back."

Miranda wanted to protest that he, more than she, should shed his wet clothes, but she realised that to do so would accomplish nothing. Besides, she wanted nothing so much as to leave this beautiful little canyon and return to the hacienda where at least she could be alone with her thoughts. Even Lucy seemed to sense that there was no point in arguing, and after Miranda had shed her shirt and jeans behind the Landrover and wrapped herself sarongwise in the roughly woven rug Rafael had handed to her, they climbed into the vehicle and began the precarious journey home.

Miranda couldn't help but notice that Rafael coughed more on the homeward journey, and during that period of negotiating the narrow pass he began to shiver in the chill air. She wanted to say something, anything to show that she cared what happened to him regardless of whether he cared what happened to her, but one look at his set countenance was sufficient to silence any sympathetic remark she might have made.

They came down into the valley just before noon and Rafael accelerated swiftly through the village and up to the hacienda, paying scarce attention to the greetings that were called to him. A strange car was standing in the courtyard when he stood on his brakes by the fountain but if he recognised it he made no comment and merely waited impatiently for them to climb down. Then with a curt: *"Adios!"* he drove away, and it wasn't until Miranda turned to mount the steps in her makeshift sarong that she remembered her shirt and jeans were still in the back of the Landrover. Her nerves tightened. She hoped she met no one in this state.

Lucy accompanied her up the steps in silence, her small face mutinous, and Miranda made no attempt to reason with her. The whole morning had been a disaster and she felt sick at heart. When they entered the imposing entrance hall, Lucy ran off, to find Juan no doubt, and Miranda turned eagerly towards the stairs.

"Señorita Lord!"

The shocked tones of Rafael's mother arrested her, and she turned reluctantly to face her hostess. "*Buenos dias*, Doña Isabella."

"But what is this?" Doña Isabella ignored her greeting. "*Señorita*, what is the explanation of your attire? Where have you been? What have you been doing? Where is the little one?"

Miranda sighed, holding the rug more firmly about her breasts. "I—fell in the lake, I'm afraid."

"You—fell—in the lake?" Doña Isabella's lips thinned. "You were with Rafael?"

"Yes." Miranda paused. "You—knew we were going to the lake? Jezebel delivered the message?"

Doña Isabella nodded curtly. "So—where is my son?"

"I—I'm afraid he's gone, *señora*. You see, he was wet, too."

"Rafael was wet?" Doña Isabella's fingers clenched. Clearly she was impatient to know every detail of this disturbing affair. "You will please to tell me how my son is wet also."

Miranda sighed. "Of course. But couldn't I go and change first, *señora*?" She looked down at the rough folds of wool that chafed her skin. "This rug is very—uncomfortable. And damp."

Doña Isabella stared at her coldly. She obviously cared little for Miranda's comfort, but her innate sense of courtesy restrained the retort that trembled on her lips. "Very well," she agreed at last. "But you must come down quickly and tell me what happened. We have guests. My son's fiancée, Señorita Vargas, and her parents are visiting us. It would not do for you to discuss such things in their presence."

123

"No, Doña Isabella."

"And the little one? She has been taken back to the *monasterio*?"

"No." Miranda shook her head. "I think she went to find Ju—that is, Don Juan, *señora.*"

Doña Isabella clicked her tongue angrily. "Oh, but this is most annoying! I must go and find her immediately. She cannot be permitted to disrupt my son's conversation with his fiancée and her parents. I will go and find her. Diaz must take her back to the *monasterio.*"

"Oh, but—" Miranda put out an appealing hand. "Could—couldn't Lucy and I have lunch together—in my room? I mean, it would give us more time alone together—to get to know one another."

Doña Isabella considered this request and then she nodded. "I do not see why not," she admitted grudgingly. "Indeed, it might solve the problem. Juan is sure to want the child to stay, whereas Valentina may have other ideas. And besides, her parents would not approve of such a situation. No—no, I think that will do very well, *señorita.*"

"Thank you, *señora.*"

It was a minor concession, but as Miranda shed the irritating folds of the rug and showered in the luxuriously appointed bathroom she half hoped Juan would refuse his permission. Somehow she doubted that Lucy would find her a suitable substitute for Tio Juan, and after this morning's events, Miranda's nerves felt shot to pieces.

CHAPTER EIGHT

WHEN Miranda came downstairs again some fifteen minutes later, neatly dressed in a plain blue cotton skirt and a white blouse, her hair secured with the tortoise-shell comb, one of the Indian maids was awaiting her in the hall.

"Doña Isabella send me to fetch you, *señorita*," she said, in heavily accented tones. "You come?"

Doña Isabella and Lucy were in a small reception lounge, and when Miranda appeared the older woman dismissed the maid and said: "Lucy has told me what happened, *señorita*."

Miranda looked at the child's rather smug expression. "Has she?"

"Yes, *señorita*. Unfortunately she has told everyone —including my son's guests."

Miranda shrugged. "I'm sorry."

"It would seem you have been most careless, *señorita*. It is fortunate that my son was there to save you."

Miranda's dark brows drew together and she looked again at Lucy, who was innocently watching the antics of a fly caught in the rays of the sun through the slatted blinds. "I—I don't know what Lucy has told you, *señora*," she ventured quietly, "but I was not in need of rescuing. I'm quite an adequate swimmer. It was all a misunderstanding."

Doña Isabella looked sceptical. "That is hardly my conception of the facts. But I do not wish to argue with you, *señorita*. Sufficient to say that your behaviour has caused a certain amount of embarrassment to my son— to *both* my sons—and it would be as well if you kept to your room for the remainder of the day."

Miranda could feel her cheeks burning. She felt like a reprimanded child and she wished that Doña Isabella could have chosen a more suitable time to speak to her when Lucy was not present. She was quite sure the little girl was finding all this vastly entertaining.

"Very well, *señora*," she managed now. "Is that all?"

Doña Isabella looked down at Lucy. "No. I have spoken to my son and he has given permission for Lucy to take lunch with you in your room. Afterwards she will be driven back to the *monasterio*."

Now it was Lucy's turn to look disconcerted. "Oh, but Tia Isabella—" she exclaimed, only to be silenced by the look of reproval on Doña Isabella's face.

"It is settled, Lucy," said the older woman firmly. "And now, you will excuse me. I must get back to my son and our guests."

Left alone, Lucy fidgeted restlessly, avoiding Miranda's eyes. Miranda watched her for a few minutes, and then she said: "Well? Shall we go upstairs? As we've both been banished from the lunch table?"

Lucy looked up at her warily. "Aren't you cross with me?"

Miranda put her hands on her hips. "Now why should I be cross with you, Lucy?"

Lucy coloured. "I don't know. I—I just thought you might be."

"What you really mean is, you've been making up stories and you're afraid I might decide to punish you for it, don't you?"

"No." Lucy hunched her shoulders. "I only said that you had fallen off the log and that Tio Rafael had rescued you."

"Is that all?" Miranda took her by the shoulders and looked squarely into her troubled face. "Is that really all?"

Lucy shifted uncomfortably. "Yes."

"Are you sure?"

126

"Yes. At least—well, I—did say that you—that you—"

"That I what?" Miranda was impatient.

"I just said that—that you shouted for help!"

"Oh, *Lucy*!" Miranda was horrified. "You know that's not true."

Lucy sniffed unhappily. "Well! You might have done, mightn't you? And—and Tio Rafael did carry you back to the shore, didn't he?"

Miranda shook her head. "No wonder Doña Isabella looked so annoyed. No doubt she thinks I fell in deliberately."

"Why should she think that?" Lucy looked puzzled.

"Oh, never mind." Miranda felt a sense of resignation. "Well, shall we go and have lunch together? We might as well. We don't seem to have a lot to say to one another otherwise."

Iñez served their meal on Miranda's balcony. It was very pleasant sitting there in the shade of the eaves eating shellfish served with a crisp salad followed by fruit and cheese and strong black coffee. Miranda spoke little during the course of the meal, but she was conscious of Lucy's eyes upon her several times and wondered what the little girl was thinking now.

When Iñez had taken their plates away, Lucy slipped off her chair and wandered curiously round the room. She fingered Miranda's brush and comb on the vanity unit and unscrewed a jar of skin perfume, inhaling its fragrance.

"This is a lovely room, isn't it?" she said, speaking voluntarily for the first time.

Miranda tried not to feel too encouraged. "It's all right," she conceded indifferently. "I'm used to something a lot less opulent."

"Opulent? What's that?"

"Oh—luxurious, expensive. I'm used to more modest surroundings."

Lucy wrinkled her nose. "In England?"

"Of course."

"You live in London, don't you?"

"Yes." Miranda was cautious.

"I know. Tio Rafael told me."

"Tio Rafael?"

"Yes. This morning, at the lake. He was telling me that people come from all over the world to see London. He talked about Buckingham Palace where the Queen lives. I've seen the Queen, haven't I?"

"Y—e—s."

"I know." Lucy tossed her head. "I told Tio Rafael I had."

Miranda licked her lips. "Do you remember that?" she ventured tentatively.

Lucy sniffed. "Of course."

Miranda drew an unsteady breath, hardly daring to go on in case she destroyed this tenuous beginning. "Do—do you remember who you were with when you saw the Queen?" she asked gently.

Lucy frowned, obviously thinking hard. Then she shook her head and Miranda's hopes scattered. "No." She pulled inquisitively at a drawer, her eyes widening when she saw the scraps of nylon underwear it contained. "Are these yours?"

"Yes." Miranda tried to hide her disappointment. What was the use? She was getting nowhere.

Lucy closed the drawer again. "I'd like some underclothes like that," she murmured wistfully.

Miranda bit her lip. Then she thought of the photographs in her handbag and determination spurred her on.

"Lucy! Bring my bag here, would you?"

It was easier than Miranda had expected. The little girl hovered beside her after bringing her the bag, clearly curious to know why Miranda had wanted it. With trembling fingers, Miranda extracted the wallet of photographs she carried with her and began to flip

128

through them. As she had expected, Lucy's curiosity got the better of her and she peered over Miranda's shoulder.

"That—that's me!" she exclaimed at last.

"That's right." Miranda tried to sound casual.

Lucy drew back. "Why are you showing them to me?"

Miranda shrugged. "I'm not. Nobody asked you to look."

Lucy considered this, her fingers plucking nervously at her dress. Then she looked down at the photograph that was presently occupying the top of the pile. She stared at it for several seconds and a troubled expression crossed her face. But no sign of recognition.

Miranda sighed. Was she doing this all wrong? Could the shock of seeing photographs of her parents do more harm than good? She wished she knew.

Lucy pointed to the photograph. "Who—who is that?" she asked reluctantly.

Miranda hesitated. "That—that's my sister, Lucy."

"Your sister?" Lucy pressed her lips together. "You mean, that's the lady who you said was—was my mummy?"

Miranda bent her head. "Yes."

Lucy began to tremble. "Well—well, I don't know her."

"That's all right." Miranda gathered the photographs together, half wishing she had never begun this.

"It's not all right." Lucy twisted her hands together. "I—I should know her, shouldn't I? If she's my mummy?"

"Calm down, Lucy." Miranda thrust the wallet back into her handbag. "Come along. I'll show you something I brought for you."

Lucy was distracted for a moment. "Something you brought for me?" she murmured. Then she looked back at the handbag. "I—I want to look at the other photographs first."

Miranda sighed again. "I don't think that's a good idea right now."

"Why not?"

Miranda shook her head. "Let me show you what I've brought for you first. It's a little pendant—"

"No. I want to see all the photographs." Lucy bent and picked up the handbag. "Go on, show me!"

Miranda opened the wallet again with reluctance, but Lucy snatched the snapshots out of her hand and began to look through them with trembling fingers, crumpling the corners in her haste. Watching her face, Miranda could see that none of them seemed to arouse any feeling of identification, and she could see the child's confidence waning. And then suddenly, her eyes brightened and she clutched one of the pictures to her for a moment before looking at it again.

"Th—there!" she stammered, thrusting it at Miranda. "Th—that—that's Fluffy, isn't it?" and she burst into tears.

Miranda looked down at the photograph of a little girl holding a small white kitten and a swelling feeling of excitement made her feel slightly sick.

"You—remember—the kitten?" she whispered. "Your kitten?"

Lucy nodded, sobbing uncontrollably.

"You know this is you with Fluffy, don't you?"

Lucy nodded again. "Wh—when—when I—I was a—a little girl—girl," she sobbed.

"That's right." Miranda drew a deep breath. "Do you remember anything else?"

Lucy shook her head. "N—no."

"Well, never mind." Miranda tried to be positive about this. "Dry your eyes. It's a beginning anyway. At least you remember Fluffy."

Lucy rubbed her eyes with the back of her hands, accepting a paper tissue from Miranda and taking the photograph again to stare at it. "Wh—where is Fluffy?"

she asked at last.

Miranda had been half dreading that question. "He—he's in England," she said casually.

"W—with Mummy and—and Daddy?"

"No." Miranda shook her head. "He lives with a Mrs Cross now."

Lucy frowned. "But he's mine!"

"I know, love. But—well, you were going away, and you can't take cats out of the country unless you want to leave them in quarantine for months and months after you get back."

"What does that mean?"

"Well, when you take a cat or a dog—any animal—out of England you have to leave it in sort of boarding kennels when you come back. You see, there are strict rules about things like that. And besides, if you had brought Fluffy to South America he might have caught some horrible disease and died."

Lucy nodded slowly. "But he's there for when I get back?"

Miranda almost gasped. "Well, I—I suppose he could be."

Lucy scuffed her toe, almost completely calm again now. "That's good," she said absently. "I should like a pet."

Miranda, who had never dreamed a breakthrough could be made so easily, was tempted to promise Lucy that she could have half a dozen assorted pets if she would agree to come back to England. But she didn't. Bribery was no better a basis for a beginning than brute force would have been, and besides, she was beginning to think that perhaps Rafael was right after all. She had been trying to rush things. If she could just give Lucy a little more time, she might achieve everything. And in her heart of hearts she knew that the finality of leaving the valley—and Rafael—was something she didn't want to have to face just yet . . .

131

Lucy asked if she could take the photograph of herself and Fluffy back to the monastery to show Father Esteban. Miranda agreed, of course, and was half relieved that the little girl did not see Juan before leaving. She would have hated for him to scoff at her small triumph.

The rest of the afternoon Miranda spent in her room. From time to time she heard the sound of voices on the patio, but they were too far away for her to distinguish who was speaking. She wondered if Rafael might be invited for dinner as they had guests, but although the prospect of seeing him again filled her with trepidation she was disappointed when Iñez came to inform her that she was expected to have dinner in her room. However, Constancia appeared in the early evening and she dispelled Miranda's doubts on that score.

"Mama is most angry with Rafael," she remarked, doing as Lucy had done and examining the various jars and bottles on the vanity unit. "Twice he has been to the hacienda without attempting to speak with her, and this afternoon, when she sent Diaz with a message inviting him to join us for dinner this evening, he sent a reply that it was *impossible*!"

Miranda linked her fingers together. "So—he is not coming?"

"No. Mama has asked Father Domenico to join us once more. He seldom refuses."

"I see."

Constancia moved impatiently about the room, small and slender in her gown of turquoise silk. Then she halted abruptly and said: "Tell me, *señorita*, did Rafael really save your life this morning?"

Miranda flushed. "Not—not really."

"But he did pull you out of the lake, *verdad*?"

"I suppose so."

Constancia shook her head. "Mama was most angry about that, also. You see, Rafael, he has always—*avoided* such situations."

132

Miranda stared at her, willing her to go on and explain that remark. But Constancia, like Carla, seemed to think that what she had said was explanation enough. With a sigh, the Mexican girl walked towards the door.

"Did you have any success with the *niña*?" she enquired, in parting.

Miranda hesitated. "A—a little."

Constancia lingered. *"Qué?"*

"I—I showed her some photographs. She recognised a kitten—a small cat—a pet she used to have in England."

"Asi?" Constancia sounded impressed. "Was that all she remembered?"

Miranda nodded. "I'm afraid so."

"No obstante, it is a beginning." Constancia smiled. "I will tell Juan the good news."

"No! That is—I'd rather you didn't," Miranda finished lamely. "Let—let Lucy tell him herself."

"A fondo." Constancia struggled. "I will say nothing." She glanced at the slim gold watch on her wrist. *"Se hace tarde.* I must go. *Adios, señorita*—until tomorrow."

But later that night, Miranda lay sleepless between the silken sheets of the luxurious bed. It had been such an eventful day, the most eventful day since her arrival here, and she was finding it impossible to empty her mind of the images that plagued it.

Her minor success with Lucy was important, of course. A beginning had been made, as Constancia had said, and it was possible that now a crack had appeared it might widen into full awareness of her identity. But it was not her success with Lucy which was driving away the waves of Morpheus.

Time and again she relived those moments on the shore of the lake when Rafael had looked down into her eyes and allowed naked passion to darken his. What had happened? Surely she had not been mistaken in thinking

133

that for a few seconds at least he had desired her—had become aware of her body and been unable to suppress the urgent needs of his own . . .

A shudder passed through her, and she sat up in bed, pressing her updrawn knees to her stomach. He had been so angry afterwards, so furious and contemptuous, not just with her but with himself. But why? Surely what had happened had been a natural enough occurrence. She was not naïve enough to imagine that every time a man showed his attraction for a woman it involved any emotional commitment on his behalf. And just because she was becoming emotionally involved with him it did not necessarily generate any similar involvement on his part . . .

She slid out of bed, wrapping her robe about her, and opened the balcony doors. Outside the air was cool and sweet, a faint breeze carrying the sounds of the tumbling river up to her. Down the valley there were no lights, nothing to be seen but the shadowy darkness splashed here and there with the ghostly pallor of colour-washed walls. And somewhere down there was Rafael's house. Was he sleeping, was he relaxing on some narrow bunk? Or was he, like her, troubled by uneasy thoughts? She doubted the latter. His life was too full, so absorbing for him to expend his energies in worry about an incident which he had no doubt forgotten by now.

With a heavy heart she closed the doors and turned back to the bed. As she shed her gown she thought that tomorrow she must write a letter to David and explain that things were taking a little longer than she had expected. She would ask for an extra week to sort out her affairs. Surely he would permit her that . . .

The next morning, Miranda met Juan's fiancée, Valentina Vargas.

The other girl was with Juan on the patio when Miranda came downstairs after taking breakfast in her room as usual. An older woman was there, too, and Miranda guessed they were being chaperoned by the girl's mother.

Miranda was reluctant to join them. She had come in search of Juan with the intention of suggesting that perhaps Diaz might be permitted to drive her to the monastery to see Lucy, but as soon as he saw her hovering uncertainly just inside the french doors, Juan sprang to his feet and performed the introductions with something closely approaching relief. Miranda hazarded that he found it difficult to relax with his fiancée when her mother could hear every word they said and there was no fourth person to distract her attention.

All the same, Miranda had no desire to be used as a buffer between Juan and his future in-laws. However, without being rude she could not refuse to take one of the basketwoven chairs he offered and accept a cup of coffee. So she sat down rather gingerly and hoped that either Doña Isabella or Constancia, or even Carla, would appear to relieve her.

Both Señora Vargas and her daughter were typically Spanish in appearance and dress, and Miranda felt conspicuous in her white jeans and purple tee-shirt. But most of her clothes were of the casual variety and she had not expected to have to share coffee with two immaculately-clad strangers. Indeed, if she had thought about the Vargas family at all, she would have expected them to have left the previous evening. Although, she reflected, she might have known that visitors did not make fleeting calls in this mountainous area.

When coffee was served and Juan had resumed his seat again, Señora Vargas turned to her and said: "You are the aunt of the child we met yesterday, *señorita*?"

"Yes, that's right."

Miranda forced a smile, but there was no answering smile in either of the two magnolia-pale faces confronting her. The two faces were very much alike—both

135

patrician in cast, both rather bland in expression—and framed by night-dark hair that formed a widow's peak above smooth foreheads.

"And when do you propose to take the child back to England, *señorita*?" Señora Vargas continued.

Miranda glanced uncomfortably towards Juan. "As soon as possible, *señora*. I—things have been complicated by the fact that Lucy doesn't remember anything."

"So I understand from Doña Isabella." Señora Vargas frowned, and then turned to Juan. "What I cannot understand is why the child should spend so much time here. Why, indeed, Señorita Lord is staying here."

Miranda's cheeks burned with embarrassment, but Juan came swiftly to her defence. "Señorita Lord is our guest, Doña Maria. Is our wish she stay here."

Señora Vargas shook her head. "Surely the affair is that of the authorities, *verdad*?"

"I make it my affair, Doña Maria," replied Juan firmly. "The *niña* she is—how you say?—delightful, *no*?"

"What Juan means, Mama, is that he is—fond of the child," said Valentina, speaking for the first time since her introduction to Miranda.

Señora Vargas's frown deepened. "Fond of the child?" she echoed. "What means this, Juan?"

Miranda sensed that Juan was getting into difficult waters as he nodded and said: "I am fond of her, *si*. I tell Valentina so."

Señora Vargas gave an impatient ejaculation. "It is time perhaps, Juan, that you had children of your own to be—*fond* of." There was a wealth of scorn in that single word.

Juan shrugged his stocky shoulders. "Is not harmful to care for the *niña*, Dona Maria. She is—*vulnerable*."

"I think what—Don Juan is trying to convey is that before I came Lucy had no one," ventured Miranda

136

tentatively. "He's been very kind to her, and she's very fond of him, too."

Señora Vargas turned cold eyes in her direction. "I think my future son-in-law is capable of making his position clear, *gracias, señorita,*" she said.

Miranda picked up her cup and swallowed some of the coffee. It was either that or say something she would no doubt regret later. All the same, she could find it in her heart to pity Juan if Valentina turned out anything like her mother in later years.

Señora Vargas returned her attention to Juan, but he spoke to Miranda before she could recommence the attack.

"You wish to see me, *señorita*?" he suggested politely.

Miranda put down her cup. "Well, yes. I—I wondered whether Diaz might run me over to the monastery this morning. As—as you have guests, *señor*." This latter consideration had only just occurred to her, but it helped to strengthen her suggestion, she thought.

It was Juan's turn to look annoyed now. "Diaz will bring the *niña* to the hacienda *por usual, señorita,*" he essayed firmly.

"*No!*" Valentina's fingers clasped his wrist. "You promised to take me riding, Juan. Let the *señorita* go to the *monasterio, caro*. It would be much more suitable."

Miranda knew that Juan must be doing battle with himself—whether to follow his own inclinations and risk alienating his fiancée's affections, or to fall in with Valentina's wishes, thereby giving Miranda a free hand. It could not be an easy decision for him.

"Valentina is right, Juan," Señora Vargas stated, with emphasis. "You two have had so little time to spend together. It is not seemly that this child—this intruder—should be allowed to interfere with your arrangements. Tell Señorita Lord she may go the *monasterio*. The sooner this situation is resolved the better."

Juan was silent for a long moment and then he covered

Valentina's hand with his own. "Very well, *amada*. Señorita Lord shall go to the *monasterio* as she wishes. But she may bring the *niña* back for lunch, *no*?"

Valentina accepted the condition, but Miranda sensed that the other girl did so under protest. It made her realise that Lucy's future here in the valley was not a realistic proposition, and that sooner or later Juan must be made to accept this. If he married Valentina there would be no place in the household for an orphaned English girl.

This knowledge strengthened Miranda's determination to win Lucy's affections all over again, and after the previous afternoon's events, Lucy was more willing to accept her aunt as someone who, far from threatening her, had her wellbeing at heart.

They spent the morning in the grounds of the monastery, running about and playing ball games, and hiding in the old graveyard that clung to the hillside behind the crumbling walls. Diaz, who had returned to the hacienda after bringing Miranda to the monastery, did not appear at lunchtime and Father Esteban insisted that they join him for the simple meal. Over cornbread and fruit, washed down by more of the goat's milk which Miranda had tried the day before, he and Miranda discussed the miraculous escape Lucy must have made. The old priest went over everything he had written in his letters to her, forgetting as the old are apt to do, that Miranda had heard it all before. Diaz eventually returned at four o'clock with a message that Lucy was not expected to visit the hacienda that day. Miranda drove away with him reluctantly, conscious of Lucy's disappointed little face all the way back to the hacienda.

She encountered one of the twins in the hall. She thought at first it was Constancia and called out a greeting, but when the girl turned she saw it was Carla. The Mexican girl's eyebrows rose at the grass-smeared appearance Miranda presented, and she commented

138

languidly: "Have you been tumbling in the hay, *señorita*? You look—dishevelled."

Miranda squashed an angry retort and replied: "I've been playing games with Lucy, *señorita*, and I don't particularly care how I look."

"Do you not, *señorita*? Why is that, I wonder? Because one of my brothers is engrossed with his so-beautiful fiancée, while the other is engrossed with—shall we say—other matters?"

Miranda walked towards the stairs. She would not enter into an argument with Carla. All the same, she longed to be able to ask her exactly what she meant by—other matters.

"Have you seen Rafael today?" queried Carla, as Miranda began to mount the stairs.

Miranda paused. "No."

"No, I thought not." Carla frowned. "No one seems to have seen Rafael since your unfortunate trip to the lake, *verdad*?"

Miranda's lips parted. "Are you trying to say something, *señorita*?"

Carla shrugged, her expression one of assumed innocence. "What might I be trying to say, *señorita*?" she countered. "No, I am—concerned about my brother, that is all. But do not let me detain you. I am sure you are eager to—to make yourself presentable again."

Miranda's clenched fists betrayed her indignation, but biting her tongue, she continued on her way upstairs and didn't realise until she expelled her breath in her room that she had been holding it.

As she bathed, however, certain of the things Carla had said came back to trouble her. Had no one seen Rafael since yesterday morning? She had half expected Carla to denounce the fact that Rafael had returned her shirt and jeans, but obviously he had not. She recalled the congestion he had said he had and his subsequent soaking in his efforts to rescue her. Surely if he was ill he

139

would have sent some word to the hacienda, to his mother at least.

But would he? Recalling his independence, the way his mother had had to plead with him to ensure his company for dinner that evening several nights ago, Miranda doubted that he would worry her with his problems. But what if he was ill and alone in that stone house by the river? Who was there to care for him? Who would ensure that he had food to eat, and fresh sheets on his bed?

Miranda stood up and reached for the fluffy bath-sheet to wrap around her. Suddenly the luxury of her surroundings were distasteful to her. She ached with the desire to know whether Rafael was all right, whether she was exaggerating the importance of that racking cough he had had. Tomorrow, she told herself determinedly, as she rubbed herself dry. Tomorrow she would find out one way or the other. When Diaz took her to the monastery, as no doubt Señora Vargas would see he did, she would ask him to call at Rafael's house first.

CHAPTER NINE

UNFORTUNATELY, Miranda did not go to the monastery next morning. Diaz had been despatched before any objections could be voiced and when Miranda went downstairs after breakfasting in her room she found Lucy already ensconced on Juan's knee at the table on the patio, eating fresh melon from his plate. Neither Valentina nor her mother were about, but an older man Miranda had not seen before was seated at the opposite side of the table, laughing at Lucy's antics. She suspected that this might be Valentina's father, a supposition which was confirmed by Juan's introduction.

"Will you not join us, *señorita*?" requested Señor Vargas smilingly, clearly not sharing his wife's aversion for an unconventionally attired English girl.

Miranda hesitated, looking at Lucy. "I—well, thank you. But I didn't expect to find you here, Lucy."

Lucy, who had had to slide off Juan's knee while he performed the introductions, shrugged her small shoulders. "I knew Tio Juan would want to see me today," she declared confidently. "I 'spect Diaz made a mistake yesterday, didn't he, Tio Juan?"

Juan looked down at her gently. "Let us say—a misunderstanding, *chica*. But no matter—you are here now, *si*?"

Lucy smiled up at him and Miranda sighed. Yesterday had been an unexpected concession. Today she would have to compete with Juan again, and Lucy was feminine enough to prefer the company of a male to that of a female.

Miranda accepted coffee and responded politely to Señor Vargas's questions about her life in England. She admitted that, apart from Lucy, she was alone in the world, that she lived in a small flat in Chelsea, and that she was secretary to a merchant banker. Clearly her replies shocked the old *hidalgo*, but he managed not to show his concern at her lack of chaperonage too obviously.

It was Juan, when she told him that she had a letter which she wished despatching to England, who said: "*Oiga*, you are not leaving, *señorita*?" in horrified tones. Even Lucy looked up at this and Miranda was warmed by the anxiety in her eyes. But whether it was at the thought of her aunt's departure or concern that she might be expected to go with her, Miranda could not be sure.

"No," she answered now, shaking her head at Juan. "As—as a matter of fact, I've asked my employer for an extra week's leave. Don Rafael said—that is, would *you* object to my staying a few more days, *señor*?"

"*Me*?" Juan made a dismissing gesture. "*Mas, no!* You know you are welcome here, *señorita*."

"Thank you." Miranda breathed a sigh of relief and Lucy resumed eating her melon.

Señor Vargas swallowed the remains of his coffee and looked at the other man. "I understand that Rafael is still here, Juan," he stated thoughtfully. "We expected he would have returned to Mexico City, *ya*?"

Miranda tried not to appear too intent on Juan's reply. "Mama is loath to let him go, Don Carlos," he said, shrugging. "So long as he is here, she has hopes of—persuasion, *no*?"

Señor Vargas looked troubled. "But is this likely?" he exclaimed, and then made an apologetic gesture towards Miranda. "I am sorry, *señorita*, I am most impolite. Forgive me. Juan and I will discuss this some other time, eh Juan?"

Juan inclined his head and the older man rose to his feet. "Excuse me, will you not? I must go and attend on my wife. No doubt I will see you again, *señorita*."

Miranda smiled and he saluted and walked away. After he had gone there was silence for a while and then Juan broke it with a startling comment: "You do not—how you say?—envy me, *señorita, no*?"

Miranda looked at him in surprise. "I don't know what you mean."

"You think is going to be *difícil*—the life with Valentina, *si*?"

Miranda coloured. "I'm sure I've never thought about it, *señor*."

"*No?*" Juan shrugged in continental fashion. "But I am doing much thinking. Do you think Valentina likes Lucy?"

Miranda made a helpless movement of her hands. "*Señor*, it's nothing to do with me!"

Juan frowned, shredding the skin of the melon with his knife. "*Verdad?* I might—disagree, *señorita*."

"What do you mean?" Miranda was completely at sea.

Juan looked at Lucy who had finished her melon and was watching them with wide eyes. "*Vaya*, Lucy. Go and play. I wish to speak with privacy to your aunt, *si*?"

Lucy pouted. "Can't I stay, Tio Juan?" she asked appealingly. "I won't listen, I promise."

Juan had to smile at this. "*No, chica*. Five minutes only. *Mire*, you may take my watch and count the minutes, *no*?"

Miranda was horrified when he unstrapped the expensive gold watch from his wrist and handed it to the child, but Lucy was entranced. And well she might be, thought Miranda ironically, realising that to Juan Cueras a watch worth several hundreds of pounds was merely a very small item. Lucy went off with the watch, well pleased, and Juan turned his full attention on Miranda.

"*Ahora, señorita*, we are alone. We can talk."

"Yes, *señor*?" Miranda was wary.

"Si." Juan pushed his plate aside and stretched a hand across the table to capture one of Miranda's. She was so astounded at this unexpected action that she didn't immediately draw her fingers away, and encouraged by her lack of protest, he said huskily: *"Señorita,* what would you say if I tell you I find you—*encantador*—enchanting, *no?"*

Miranda snatched her hand away, pressing it into the palm of the other that rested rather nervously now in her lap. "I—I can't imagine why you're saying such things to me when your fiancée may appear at any moment!" she exclaimed.

Juan squared his shoulders. "And if I care not what Valentina may see?"

Miranda caught her breath. "I don't understand you, *señor."*

Juan's eyes bored into hers. "Do you not, *señorita?* I think you do." He paused. "Miranda. Is a beautiful name, *no?* Miranda—Cueras! Do you think that sounds even better?"

Miranda got to her feet. She was trembling. "I—I think you're teasing me, *señor.* If—if that's all you have to say, I'll go and find Lucy—"

"Ah, Lucy." Juan lay back in his chair looking up at her. "Dear little Lucy! Would you not like to solve her problems and your own together?"

"Señor, I really think—"

"Si. Think!" Juan sprang to his feet, approaching her determinedly. "Think Miranda. You do not take me—*seriamente,* I think." Although she had backed away from him he caught both her hands in his, holding them tightly in his moist fingers. "I mean what I say, *cara.* I think I am in love with you."

Miranda gasped, and with a desperate effort freed herself, putting the width of the glass-topped table between them. *"Señor,* I don't know what your game is—"

"Game? Is no game, Miranda. I want to marry you."

Miranda breathed deeply. "You're not serious!"

"I am. I am. Can you not see that I am telling you the truth?"

Miranda clutched at straws. "You're doing this for Lucy. It's Lucy you want."

Juan shrugged. "I admit—I care for the child. But marriage is more—much more than making babies, *no*?"

Miranda's cheeks flamed. "I—I—" She felt tongue-tied. "I'm—sorry—"

"Sorry?" Juan frowned. *"Por qué?"*

Miranda shook her head helplessly and at that moment Carla came strolling on to the patio, dressed as she frequently was in riding clothes. Her expression was as composed as ever, but Miranda wondered uneasily how she could have failed to overhear at least part of their conversation. Certainly she gave no indication of it as she turned to her brother.

"Valdez is waiting in the hall, Juan," she advised him crisply. "You had better go and speak with him. Apparently a cat has been driven down from the mountains by the rains and has killed a number of cattle."

Juan uttered an imprecation and looked regretfully at Miranda. *"Qué fastidio!"* he sighed. *"Muy bien,* I will speak with him. Wait for me, Miranda."

After he had left them Carla's eyes fastened on Miranda's hot cheeks. "So," she murmured. "I was right, *señorita.*"

"You weren't right," retorted Miranda, feeling slightly sick. "I—your brother is making a terrible mistake."

Carla's eyes narrowed. "He will not be allowed to make it."

"Well, that suits me," muttered Miranda.

"So—when are you leaving, *señorita*?"

"Leaving?" Miranda shook her head. "I don't know. As soon as possible, I suppose." She moved vaguely towards the gardens, needing time to think—to be alone—to dismiss Juan's preposterous proposition from her thoughts. "Er—I must find Lucy," she said abruptly, and walked quickly away.

As luck would have it matters of the estate occupied Juan for the rest of the morning and at lunch time Doña Isabella was more than willing to grant permission for Lucy to share Miranda's meal in her room. Lucy was not enthusiastic. She had wanted to return Juan's watch. But Doña Isabella saw it and took charge of it, assuring the child that she would see that Juan gained possession of it once more.

After lunch, Juan sent a message asking Lucy and Miranda to join him on the patio.

Lucy was delighted, but Miranda said she had a headache and asked Lucy to make her apologies for her non-appearance.

"But you were all right five minutes ago!" exclaimed the little girl, lingering by the door where Iñez waited to escort her, perceptive enough to realise that her adopted uncle would not be pleased at Miranda's refusal.

"It's just come on," lied Miranda, turning her revealing face away. "I'll be all right if I rest for a while."

Lucy hesitated a moment longer and then with a shrug she left her. After she had gone, Miranda breathed a sigh of relief and began to pace restlessly about the room. She was still by no means decided over what she could do about Juan's proposal, and while she told herself that he had not been serious, that he already had a fiancée who would not relinquish him so carelessly, she could not dismiss his determination to gain control of Lucy. Since their conversation that morning, she had pondered the possibility that Lucy had told him about recognising the kitten in the snapshot, thus convincing him that her memory was returning gradually. But would he ask her, Miranda, to marry him just to retain his hold on the child? He couldn't really be in love with her, could he? She shook her head miserably. She had the disturbing feeling that they were in the clutches of a petulant child who would do anything—promise anything—to get his own way. If only Rafael had been the one . . .

She wrapped her arms closely about herself. Rafael! But this situation would never have arisen with Rafael. He simply wasn't interested in her in that way—in *any* way.

She stared dejectedly out of her windows, looking down the valley, as though by the pure concentration of her thoughts she could summon his image to sight. But no Landrover appeared to climb the hill towards the hacienda, and her spirits drooped. Where was Rafael? Why didn't he come? Why didn't he return her clothes if nothing else?

She turned back into the room and stood for a moment thinking hard. How could she get down to his house without anyone being aware of it? She could drive, but no one was likely to offer her the use of the car without some specific destination in mind. She could walk—but it was quite a long way, and she didn't want to have to come back possibly in the dark. She sighed. If only there were telephones she could use. But even her letter, which she had eventually decided to send, had had to be given to Doña Isabella for transportation to the airport and from there to Mexico City. Pony express! she thought impatiently, and then uttered a small gasp. Of course! Why hadn't she thought of it before? She could ride! And as there were horses in the stables at the back of the hacienda, there was no reason why she should not ride to the village.

She clasped her hands together. But how? How to approach the stablehands? And what if Carla or some-one else was there? But no! Carla rested in the after-noons, as did her mother and sister, and no doubt Señora Vargas and her daughter rested, too. Juan was on the patio with Lucy. She ought not to be missed for an hour or so.

She looked down at her shirt and trousers. At least they were suitable on this occasion, she thought wryly. Taking a ribbon from the drawer, she secured her hair at her nape and then after a quick glance at her reflection she left the room and went quietly down the stairs.

As she had expected, the house was unnervingly quiet, but she managed to reach the front terrace without incident and made her way in the direction of the stables. A young Indian boy was polishing some harness in the yard and he looked up in surprise when he heard Miranda's footsteps.

"Buenas tardes, señorita," he greeted her politely. *"Puedo ayudarle?"*

Miranda replied with what she hoped was a engaging smile. "I—I want a horse," she said slowly. "En—un caballe?"

"Un caballo, señorita? Ah, you wish—*ir a caballo?"*

Miranda looked doubtful and he smiled and patted a saddle close by. Then he made a motion of holding reins and she nodded. "Yes. Yes, I want to go riding."

The boy seemed pleased that they had solved their difficulties but then he hesitated. "Is—permit, *señorita?"* he asked, frowning at her obviously unaccustomed attire.

Miranda bit her lip. Then she nodded. "Don Juan has given his permission," she said, crossing her fingers behind her back.

The mention of Juan's name was sufficient to remove any lingering traces of doubt in the boy's face, and she hoped he would not be called upon to account his reasons for letting her have a mount. But why should he? she argued with herself. She would ride to the village and see Rafael, and be back before anyone became aware of her absence.

The mount the boy produced for her seemed gentle

148

enough. It was a chestnut mare with doe-like eyes and a thick swishing tail. She made no objection when Miranda climbed into the unfamiliar saddle, and at a pressure from her knees trotted obediently out of the stable yard. Miranda raised a hand in thanks to the boy and then gave her attention to the animal. So far so good.

However, once the yard was left behind, the mare seemed to find her spirit, and when Miranda tried to direct her down the track to the village she left the path and began to descend the grassy slope instead. Deciding that no doubt the animal knew the way better than she did, Miranda gave in trying to force her back on to the track again, and although they were going down at a quicker pace than she would have chosen, she was too busy holding on to worry overmuch. Below them, the river sparkled in the heat of the sun, and Miranda could feel the dampness at the back of her neck. She should have brought a scarf, she thought impatiently, and looked forward to reaching the coolness of Rafael's house.

The Chapel of the Innocents was just below them now and beyond she could see the torn slats of the bridge which had taken such a beating on the night of the storm. Further along the riverbank, she could see the white stone walls of a single-storied building and her heart lifted. Rafael's house.

However, the mare was seemingly in no hurry to reach her destination now and refused to be spurred on. She lingered at the water's edge and for a heart-stopping moment Miranda thought she was about to receive another unwelcome dipping. But the mare halted and stood sniffing the air, as though deciding what to do next.

Anger and impatience made Miranda attempt to climb down from the saddle. She thought she would lead the mare the rest of the way. But one foot was still in the nearside stirrup when the horse began to move and although Miranda tried to scramble up again, she lost her balance and fell heavily to the ground. The fall winded her, but her weight slowed the mare to a standstill again. But not before Miranda became conscious of an agonising pain in her hip.

By a great effort of willpower she managed to dislodge her foot from the stirrup and lay still for several minutes getting her breath back. The mare wandered a few yards away, cropping at the grass with seeming indifference to her plight, and when she was able Miranda propped herself up on her elbows and tried not to succumb to the tears of pain and frustration that blurred her vision.

There was no one about from whom she could have asked assistance, but an attempt to stand confirmed her worst fears. She had obviously injured her leg in some way and every step she took sent a sharp pain right up her spine. An unsuccessful attempt to catch the mare's reins brought more tears to her eyes and with a set face she turned determinedly towards Rafael's house.

By the time she reached the front entrance, she was bathed in sweat, and not only from the effort of walking in the afternoon heat. Her leg and her back were burning balls of pain and she felt sick with reaction. Rafael's Landrover was parked out front and the original reasons which had brought her here quickened her step. If he was ill, she would have to overcome her own discomfort.

The house seemed deserted and her heart pounded anxiously. Lounge, office, kitchen—all were empty. He must be in the bedroom, which meant her worst fears were realised. She stumbled along the hall opening doors—a bathroom, a broom cupboard, a room containing two beds, and finally another room containing three beds, one of which was occupied. She stood unsteadily in the doorway, listening to his heavy breathing. There was congestion there as he had said, and she put a trembling hand to her lips. Oh, God, she thought desperately, how could she help anyone in this condition?

"What are you doing here, *señorita*?"

The cool purposeful tones behind her sent Miranda teetering on her uninjured leg. "Raf—Rafael!" she gasped, hardly aware that she had used his name. She stared at his lean face as if she couldn't believe her eyes, then she looked back at the bed. "I—I thought—that was you!"

Rafael drew her outside and closed the door behind them with a definite click. "I asked what you were doing here, *señorita*," he repeated coldly.

Miranda's lips trembled. "I—I came to see you. I thought you must be ill. There—there was no word—"

Rafael's eyes narrowed and he took a few steps along the hall obviously expecting her to do the same. When she did not he came back to her, a scowl marring his attractive features. "I had work to do, *señorita*," he told her impatiently. "As you saw, there is a sick man in that room. Rodrigues has had a spate of illness since the storm."

Miranda made a gesture of acquiescence. She should not have come here. Her back was paining her abominably with standing in one position for so long, and she had no idea how she was going to get back to the hacienda. And as for capturing the mare . . . An ache was beginning somewhere near her temples and seemed to be penetrating to her nape. Realising she had to say something, she said: "That's all right, then, isn't it?" and swayed a little.

Rafael was staring at her curiously. Perhaps he had only just noticed that there were beads of perspiration on her forehead and that her cheeks were pale and drawn. He laid a hand against her forehead, and she just managed not to flinch away from his touch. His fingers felt cool, but she guessed it was her head that was burning. *"Sagrada Maria!"* he snapped huskily, "are you ill?"

151

Miranda moved her head painfully from side to side. "I—the horse—I was trying to dismount and—and it moved away—" And for the first time in her life she slid into a dead faint at his feet . . .

When she recovered consciousness, she was lying between thin cotton sheets in one of the narrow beds she had glimpsed earlier. There was another bed beside her, but it was empty, and she recalled the twin-bedded room she had looked into during her search for Rafael. Someone had removed her clothes and her body felt relaxed, but tender. She still ached, but it was a bearable thing compared to what she had suffered. She tried to move her legs and immediately became aware of vague sensations of pain hovering just beyond conscious reach.

She lay still trying to calculate what time it must be. It was still daylight outside the narrow windows, but the sun was sinking fast and soon it would be dark. A sense of dread enveloped her at the realisation that everyone must know what she had done by now, and humiliation brought her into an upright position. The action was painful, and she was fighting away waves of dizziness when the door opened.

As Rafael walked towards the bed, she pressed the sheet closely to her breasts, her cheeks darkening at the knowledge that it must have been he who had undressed her and put her to bed.

"Are you feeling better?" he enquired, standing beside the bed, looking down at her with intent eyes.

Miranda nodded. "Mu—much better, thank you. I—I'm sorry I've been such a nuisance. I'll go as soon as I can get dressed."

Rafael shook his head slowly. "You will not be going anywhere, *señorita*," he stated uncompromisingly. "You need several days of complete bed rest. You are lucky to get away so lightly. You could so easily have damaged your spine."

Miranda stared at him incredulously. "But I can't stay here!"

His eyes narrowed, the thick lashes successfully veiling his expression. "No?"

"No." She shifted restlessly, aware that the slightest movement caused her some discomfort. "I—nobody knows where I am. And Lucy is at the hacienda. I'm supposed to have a headache—to be resting—"

"You are resting, *señorita*," he observed without humour. "Do not alarm yourself. My family have been advised of your whereabouts. They have also been informed that you are in no fit state to be moved for the present. It is unfortunate, but unavoidable." His jaw hardened. "As far as I can ascertain at this time there appears to be no irreparable damage to your back, *señorita*. But the next few days will either confirm or disprove my diagnosis."

Miranda heaved a deep sigh. "I see." She looked up at him, her lips moving mutinously. "Are you very angry with me?"

Rafael frowned. "Angry, *señorita*?"

"Yes—angry." Miranda was impatient herself now. "You stand there telling me the cold facts of my condition, and all the time you must be despising me for landing myself on you, uninvited!"

Rafael thrust his hand into the high pockets of his cream corded pants. "You are a patient, *señorita*. Naturally I will do what I can for you—as I would for anyone in your position."

"Oh, *thank you!*" Miranda plucked restlessly at the sheet, her tone deliberately sarcastic, wanting to arouse him as he seemed always able to arouse her. "And I suppose I was just a patient when you picked me up and carried me in here and stripped me of my clothes, wasn't I?" she taunted, her voice rising unsteadily.

Rafael sighed. "Do not get hysterical, *señorita*. There is no shame in what I did. I am a doctor. I have examined

153

many women. I have delivered babies. You were no different from my other patients."

Miranda caught her breath on a sob. "I know. That's what I mean."

Rafael drew his hands out of his pockets and she could see they were clenched. "You must be hungry, *señorita*. I will get you some food."

Miranda remembering how she had planned to care for him, felt a terrible sense of contrition. Moving her head in a negative gesture, she caught his wrist between her fingers. "I—I'm sorry," she groaned, looking up at him through drowned pupils. "I'm sorry. I'm a bitch! I know you've done your best for me. Don't be angry with me, please!"

Rafael looked down at her hand gripping his wrist and a tormented expression crossed his lean face. "I am not angry with you, *señorita*," he declared tautly. "I realise your intentions in coming here were commendable and I appreciate them. But you are my patient now, and I will do my best to look after you."

"Oh, *Rafael*!" His name was torn from her. "Don't you ever relax your guard? Don't you ever feel any emotion?"

His eyes darkened, but whether with passion or anger she could not be certain. He wrenched his wrist out of her grasp and strode towards the door. "I will get you some soup, *señorita*," he stated bleakly, and left her.

CHAPTER TEN

DURING the next few days Miranda had to learn to suffer Rafael's impersonal examinations without embarrassment. The morning after her accident, a young Indian girl who introduced herself as Eva Mejor presented herself for duty, and it was she who cared for Miranda—changing her bed linen, supplying medication, serving meals. Miranda saw practically nothing of Rafael himself except in the early mornings when he came to examine her. Then he would strip the covers away, his face devoid of emotion, his hands cool and efficient as they probed her bruised flesh. To Miranda, who longed for those hands to caress her, to touch her in a much more personal manner, it was a bitter-sweet experience, over too soon. Then he would exchange a few words in the Mexican tongue with Eva Mejor and depart about his other business with only a curt: *"Adios, señorita!"* to last her through the day.

She had only one visitor during those few days—Constancia. The younger girl arrived on the afternoon following the accident, but it soon became apparent that she had not really wanted to come. She was ill at ease and although she enquired about Miranda's health there was a lack of enthusiasm in her attitude. Miranda couldn't understand why until at last Constancia got to the real point of her visit. Twisting her hands together, she said: "My mother does not wish you to return to the hacienda when you are recovered, *señorita.*"

Miranda managed not to show her dismay. "Oh!"

Constancia sighed unhappily. "I am sorry, *señorita.*"

Miranda shrugged. "It's not your fault." She was sitting up in bed dressed in an ugly cotton nightshirt that

155

would have been more suitable for a man twice her size. She forced a smile. "Perhaps you could arrange to have my—my belongings packed up for me. I—I could do with some pyjamas."

"I brought your things with me," admitted Constancia, her face red. "My mother insisted."

"I see." Miranda swallowed hard. So it was definite, was it? "I'm sorry she feels that way. But she has no reason to feel jealous of me—"

"Jealous of you, *señorita?*" Constancia frowned. "I do not understand."

Miranda tugged at the sheet. "I expect she thinks I am a scarlet woman or something, being here alone with Rafael—I mean, Don Rafael. She had no reason to feel so—"

"But of course!" exclaimed Constancia impatiently. "We know that. Rafael is not her concern."

"No?"

"No." Constancia shook her head. "It is Juan! Of course, I did not explain myself very well. Juan has broken his betrothal to Valentina."

"What?" Miranda was horrified. "I don't believe it."

"Unfortunately, it is so. My brother is obsessed with the child—and you, *señorita.*"

Miranda moved restlessly, wincing as she flexed the torn muscles. "I—I didn't know. I never dreamed—"

"Carla told our mother she had seen Juan making love to you on the patio."

"Carla is a mischief-maker!" Miranda made a helpless gesture. "Constancia, you've got to believe me—I didn't encourage your brother! I'm not interested in him!"

Constancia shrugged now. "It is no matter. Juan has refused to go on with the betrothal. There was a terrible row last evening and Valentina and her parents left this morning."

"Oh, no!"

"It is so, *señorita.* So you see, my mother is determined to keep you and Juan apart."

Miranda sighed. "I see. And I thought . . ." She looked down at her trembling fingers. "I seem to have become a nuisance to everybody, don't I?"

Constancia looked uncomfortable. "Not to Rafael, I am sure."

Miranda felt frustrated. "You say that so calmly—so assertively. Why not to Rafael? Isn't your mother afraid that Rafael might find me a—a temptation, too?"

Constancia's small face was grave. "Rafael is not interested in women, *señorita*, as I am sure you are aware. His bride is the church. Soon he is to return to the seminary in Mexico City where he is studying to be a priest."

It was fortunate that Eva Mejor chose that moment to come in and say apologetically that the visitor would have to leave, that her patient required further treatment. Miranda could not have said anything. She was deeply shocked and a terrifying numbness behind her eyes was giving the whole scene a curiously unreal appearance. It couldn't be true, she tried to tell herself unconvincingly, fighting the faintness which was threatening to overwhelm her. But she was still too weak to offer much resistance, and for the second time in two days she lost consciousness.

When she came round this time both Rafael and Eva were in the room, but Constancia was gone. The relief on their faces when she opened her eyes would have been comical had Rafael not spoiled it all by saying: "You are trying to do too much with too little strength, *señorita*. There will be no more visitors."

Miranda had to accept this. What other reason could there be for this terrible sense of inadequacy that engulfed her every time she tried to think of the future?

During the next couple of days she devoted all her energies to recovering her strength. She ate everything they gave her, swallowed sleeping tablets without question, and generally closed her mind to any speculation about Rafael. Only when she was near him did she find this dictate hard to adhere to. He didn't look well either, despite his apparent energies. But those times were few and far between and she managed to achieve a certain measure of detachment. She had Lucy to think of, she told herself, and as soon as she was able to walk she was going to take the child and herself out of this valley, with or without anyone else's permission.

At the end of her fifth day at the house she was able to get out of bed and walk around the bedroom. The strained muscles had responded well to Eva's massage and the complete physical rest worked its own cure. She still limped, of course, and there was no question of her being able to carry suitcases or cross an airport tarmac unaided, but she was making progress.

But as her strength increased, so too did her misery over Rafael. While she was partially sedated, living on borrowed time, existing from one sleeping draught to the next, it had been easy to tell herself that she was recovering from that particular malady. To be fully conscious, fully aware of the man who slept only a couple of doors away, was another matter.

The night after her first experience of getting up, Miranda just couldn't sleep. Her mind was too active, her thoughts too chaotic to permit her to relax. On her bedside table lay the two sleeping tablets Eva had left her before leaving that evening, but for once Miranda had decided to try and do without them. And this was the result!

Depression settling on her like a shroud, she leant across and fumbled for the tablets. Where on earth were they? It was so dark, and there was no electric light at Rafael's house, only gas lights that required lighting with matches. Her fingers struck the glass of water Eva had also left on the table, sending its contents all over the floor.

"Damn!" Miranda dragged herself upright. "Damn, damn, damn!" Even if she found the tablets now she wouldn't be able to take them without a drink.

She slid her legs out of bed. There was nothing for it but to pad along to the kitchen and boil more water. At least her eyes were accustoming themselves to the gloom now and she could see where she was going. She reached for her silk robe and wrapped it closely about her. Although she still slept in her skin she wore pyjamas during the day.

The passage was cold to her feet and she hurried down it, not wanting to disturb anyone. However, a light showed beneath the kitchen door and when she tentatively propelled it open she found Rafael seated on a wooden form by the blackened hearth, his head buried in his hands.

Her heart thumped heavily as she stared at his bent head, for the moment completely unaware of her presence. Then as though some sixth sense warned him that he was no longer alone, he looked up and saw her. She gasped at the agony she glimpsed in his face, and then it was gone. He had schooled his features into the polite mask she knew so well.

"Rafael!" she breathed unsteadily, moved to say something. "Are—are you ill? It's so late. Why aren't you in bed?"

Rafael got unsteadily to his feet and she thought for a moment that he had been drinking. And then she realised that he swayed from weariness.

"What do you want?" he enquired heavily. "I was just about to retire."

Miranda gathered her scattered emotions. She must remember that whatever ailed him it had nothing to do with her. "I—er—I knocked over my water," she managed, her voice gaining in confidence. "Do you think I might have some more?"

Rafael blinked, and raked a hand through his tousled

dark hair. "What? Oh—oh, yes, of course." His shirt was unfastened almost to his waist and he tugged absently at the hair on his chest. "I will put on the kettle."

"It's all right, I can do it."

Miranda crossed the room and they both reached simultaneously for the kettle. Rafael's fingers brushed her bare arm where the wide sleeves of her gown had fallen back and a shudder ran through him. Miranda almost snatched up the kettle and moved swiftly away to the sink where a pump handle supplied cold water. She was trembling, and a glance at his set features convinced her that he was not entirely in control of his emotions.

She filled the kettle and came back to put it on the stove. Rafael, a pulse jerking at his jawline, struck a match and lighted the gas for her, and then stood aside stiffly, like an automaton. Miranda cast another anxious look in his direction and then linking her fingers turned away. The atmosphere was taut with undercurrents of feeling but whether it was apparent to Rafael, too, she could not in all honesty say. She drew a trembling breath. Let the kettle boil quickly!

She felt rather than heard him move to stand right behind her. Through the thin material of her gown she could feel the warmth of his body, the nearness of the long powerful legs. She wanted to move away, but she felt riveted to the spot, scarcely daring to breathe in case she precipitated some irrevocable move on his part. If she stayed perfectly still, she told herself, he would not touch her.

But she was wrong. His hands curved over her shoulders almost of their own volition, she felt, and he drew her resistingly back against him. Miranda struggled, knowing he was going to hate himself for doing this and not wanting him to hate her as well, but he stifled her struggles without effort and muttered: "*Be still!*" against her neck. His mouth was like a lick of flame to her kindled emotions, his tongue a tantalising caress against her skin.

"No," she protested, trying to drag herself away from him. "Rafael, *no!*"

Her struggles only seemed to incite him, however, and his hands slid from her shoulders over her throat, her breasts, seeking and finding the warm, pliant flesh beneath her gown. She could feel the hardness of his chest and thighs and the desire to yield against him was an intoxicating temptation. But she had to keep her head . . .

"Let me go, Rafael," she implored, arching away from him. "Think what you're doing!"

"Do you think I am not thinking?" he groaned thickly, exposing the smooth flesh of her shoulder to his caressing lips. "Thinking and feeling and wanting . . . Do not fight me, Miranda. I am only human and a man can stand so much and no more. You think I am cold, unfeeling—but you are mistaken. Do you think I have never experienced the delights of a woman's body? It is not so. I will not disappoint you. My father taught me well—too well!" Bitterness had invaded his tones. "The richness of the feast made an abstainer of its most fervent devotee!"

"I don't know what you're talking about," exclaimed Miranda feverishly, continuing to fight him while her strength diminished. "You've got to let me go!"

Rafael's answer was to twist her round in his arms, crushing her cruelly against him making her wholly aware of the physical needs of his body. "Kiss me, Miranda," he commanded savagely, "kiss me, love me—cleanse me of this devil that is driving me out of my mind!"

Miranda pressed her palms against his chest, unable to prevent her nails from curling painfully into his skin. But he didn't seem to notice. She kept her chin pressed down, refusing to offer her lips for his possession. But impatience brought his hand round her throat, and his thumb forced her face up to his.

His mouth fastened itself to hers, parting her lips with an expertise that confirmed his earlier assertion of experience. But what began as a hungry assault on her body softened into a lingering intimacy, a seduction of the senses more passionate than any violent assuagement could be. His hands moved over her back, caressing her, arousing her, destroying her desire to resist him. She could feel him trembling against her and felt a ridiculous sense of triumph that she could do this to him.

But her triumph was short-lived. Rafael was swinging her up in his arms, carrying her out of the kitchen and along the hall to her bedroom. Cold reason broke through the mists of emotion. She could not go on with this. No matter how Rafael felt, what he thought about her, however he despised her independent existence, she was not accustomed to going to bed with any man, and although Rafael was the first man she had ever wanted to go to bed with common sense in the cool draught of the hall warned her of the dangers. Apart from anything else, Rafael had no intentions of making any lasting commitment, his sole desire was to possess her body and rid himself of the irritating discomfort of wanting her. A cold memory at best when she was back in England.

But it would be something to remember, her senses teased her. In the bleak years to come when she might have to marry some man she did not love, might it not be some consolation to know that once the man she loved had made love to her? But would that be the end of it? What if something happened? What if she became pregnant? Emotion stirred again. The idea of being pregnant with Rafael's child was an emotive one.

The shadows in the bedroom seemed deeper, more sharply defined, as Rafael laid her on the bed and began to tear his shirt from his trousers. But Miranda took the moment's respite to slide across the bed and get off it at the other side.

"No, Rafael!" she said determinedly, her voice unsteady. "No. I won't let you touch me!"

Rafael became still, a shadowy figure whose expression she could not see. For a few agonising seconds there was complete silence and all she could hear was her own laboured breathing. And then he uttered a tortured expression of pain and disgust, and snatching up his discarded garments left the room.

For almost five minutes after the door had closed, Miranda remained where she was, frozen into a broken statue. And then reaction set in and she flung herself upon the bed, silent sobs racking her body.

Towards the morning she fell into a restless sleep, punctuated with horrific nightmares that brought her upright in the bed, sweating with fear. However, eventually, exhaustion claimed her, and she was still sleeping when Eva Mejor arrived with her breakfast.

But with the morning came the uneasy conviction that perhaps her memories of the night before had been merely the result of an overcharged imagination. Had it really happened? Had Rafael held her in his arms and kissed her, carried her to her bedroom and attempted to make love to her—or had she dreamed it all? The empty water glass lying on the floor was small reassurance when Rafael himself appeared, as remote as ever. The usual routine of examination and discussion deviated in no way from the pattern and his touch was as impersonal as it had ever been. Did she imagine the slight darkening of his eyes as he straightened the bedcovers, and were the lines etched so grimly beside his mouth deeper than they had been the day before? She couldn't be sure, and with Eva Mejor's inquisitive eyes noting every detail of their silent interchange she had no chance to find out.

Rafael paused after his examination and said: "You

163

seem much improved, *señorita*. Maybe tomorrow we can permit you to return to the hacienda."

Miranda's lips parted. "Oh, no—that is, I can't go back there."

Rafael scowled. "Why not?"

Miranda looked meaningfully towards Eva and with a flick of his fingers Rafael dismissed the other woman. "Well?" he queried curtly.

Miranda sighed. "You know your mother doesn't want me to go back," she stated flatly.

Rafael took a step nearer the bed. "My mother does not wish you—" He broke off. "Explain yourself, *señorita*."

Miranda lay back on the pillows wearily. "Oh, Rafael, must we go on with this stupid masquerade? You know perfectly well that your mother imagines I have designs on your brother! And for goodness' sake, stop calling me *señorita!* My name is Miranda, and you know that as well as I do!"

Rafael's fists clenched. "You do not make it easy for me, do you, Miranda?" he demanded in a tortured voice. "Very well, I do think of you as Miranda, but what I do not understand is this affair of Juan and yourself. In what way are you involved with him?"

Miranda turned her face aside from the anger in his. "I am not involved with him," she declared impatiently. "Surely Constancia told you he has broken his engagement."

"*Impossible!*" Rafael stared at her. "No. Constancia did not tell me this." He shook his head. "I confess, I did not give her the opportunity. You had fainted. I had other things on my mind."

"And haven't you been up to the hacienda since I've been here?" exclaimed Miranda incredulously, turning to look at him again, but now he turned away.

"No," he admitted in a low voice. "No, I have not been to the hacienda."

164

"Oh, Rafael! But you said—when I had the accident—"

"I said that my family had been informed of your accident, and so they were. I sent a message. And since then I have had no time."

Miranda looked down at her fingers twisting the cotton sheet. "Well, anyway, that's not important now, is it? As you say, I'm much improved. I shall make arrangements for Lucy and me to leave the valley as soon as possible—"

"No!" Rafael was adamant. "No, you cannot do that."

"Why not?" Miranda looked up. "I—I have to get back. And Lucy will have to come with me. Whatever your brother says."

Rafael turned to look at her broodingly. "And what did he say to you, Miranda? Why did he break his betrothal?"

Miranda flushed. "That's not important—"

"I disagree. I want to know Miranda." He took a step nearer the bed. "Tell me! I insist."

Miranda was troubled by the impassioned penetration of his eyes. Shaking her head, she said: "Oh, it was silly—silly! He said he was in love with me. Me!" She gave a short laugh. "I didn't believe him, of course."

Rafael was breathing heavily. "I see. But you said none of this to me."

"How could I?" Miranda spread her hands. "Would you have been interested?"

Rafael had himself under rigid control. "It has been an impossible situation from the start. But naturally you will go back to the hacienda. I myself, will arrange it. And if Juan makes a nuisance of himself—"

"Oh, please, *please!* I don't want to go back there." Miranda was very nearly at the end of her tether. She drew a steadying breath. "As I've said, I shall make arrangements to leave the valley—"

"Not yet!" Rafael spoke through his teeth. "Miranda, I beg of you, do not drive me too far!"

Miranda caught her breath. "I don't know what you mean—"

"Oh, yes, you do." Rafael was pale now. For a few moments he looked at her as he had looked at her the night before and then with a harsh exclamation he moved towards the door. "I must go," he muttered thickly. "I have work to do. I—Eva will bring you your clothes and you may dress and go outside for a while. But do not leave the immediate vicinity of this house, do you understand?"

Miranda nodded, not trusting herself to speak, and he went out of the room, slamming the door behind him.

Miranda was not as strong as she had imagined. Her walk to the river and back exhausted her and she was glad of the mug of hot, milky chocolate which Eva had waiting for her on her return. The two women sat together companionably in the kitchen, but their lack of communication robbed the situation of any feeling of shared confidence. Eva's English was confined to a few sentences relating to the sickroom and any attempt at conversation left both of them at a loss.

They were still sitting there when a visitor arrived. He came striding down the hall, calling Rafael's name, and Evan sprang to her feet excitedly and said: *"Este le padre, señorita."*

A few moments later Father Domenico appeared in the doorway. "Ah, *buenos dias, señoritas. Como esta?"*

Eva replied in her own language and Miranda gave a slight smile. She had not seen the priest since the evening of the dinner party at the hacienda when they had been introduced and she suspected his motives for being here. He was a close friend of Doña Isabella and no doubt he was on business for the Cueras family.

Eva offered chocolate which he accepted and after a few words with her he seated himself opposite Miranda.

166

"Eva tells me that Rafael is not here, *señorita*. I am not sorry. I wanted to speak with you."

Miranda's fingers tightened round her beaker. "With me, *señor*?"

"*Si, señorita*. Ah, *chocolate*, Eva, *gracias*." He took the mug gratefully and the other girl, either sensing he wanted to speak privately with Miranda or having been forewarned excused herself and left them. "*Ahora, señorita*, now we can talk, *si?*"

Miranda took a sip of her chocolate before replying. "I can't imagine what we have to talk about, *señor*. If it's about Lucy and Juan, I should tell you—"

"Peace, my daughter! I did not come here to talk of your niece or her estimable benefactor. No." He shook his head. "I wish to speak with you of Rafael."

"*Rafael?*" Miranda couldn't hide her astonishment. "But—" Her cheeks burned suddenly. "What about Rafael?"

For an agonising moment she wondered if Rafael had seen the priest that morning and confessed his behaviour of the night before to him. But as Father Domenico continued she realised that if Rafael had sought absolution it was not from him.

"I am concerned about Rafael," he replied confidingly. "And I thought perhaps you, with your—shall we say objective assessment of the situation, might be able to help me."

Miranda gripped the beaker with both hands. "Yes?"

"Yes." Father Domenico paused. "It is not easy for me, *señorita*. This is a—delicate matter. But one which I feel might ultimately be of assistance to his family."

"Yes." Miranda knew she sounded naïve, but she couldn't help it. She couldn't imagine why she should have been singled out to hear his concern about Rafael. Surely Doña Isabella had not sanctioned this!

The priest drummed his fingers on the table for a moment and then stilled them. "You are aware, are you not, *señorita,* that Rafael believes he has this vocation to enter the priesthood?"

"Constancia—that is—Señorita Cueras told me."

He nodded. "So. What you may not be aware of is that his—decision—was not approved by his mother."

"No?"

"No." Father Domenico shook his head. "Rafael is the eldest son. The estate is his heritage, not Juan's. It was most distressing for his mother when he chose to ignore the responsibilities that were his."

Miranda licked her dry lips. "Perhaps—perhaps he considered these—other responsibilities more important."

Father Domenico shook his head again, impatiently. "Rafael is an idealist," he said, as though it was not a nice thing to be. "He has acquired some notion that his actions can influence the—what do you say?—status quo? *Si,* the status quo. But of course, it would need a minor revolution to do that, and one man cannot hope for so much."

"Rafael cares about the people—"

"Of course he does. The *patron* always cares about his people. That is nothing new. We constantly strive towards better conditions for the people."

"But he wants to help them—physically help them—"

"I do not deny it." The priest spread his hands, but Miranda sensed a certain impatience in him now. "Rafael is a lot like his father, and the people loved him." His lips twisted. "Too well, some might say. And Rafael would not care for the comparison. It brings back too many unwelcome recollections."

Miranda moved her shoulders uncomfortably. "I really don't think you should be discussing Raf—Don Rafael's private affairs with me."

"No?" The priest's eyes were very penetrating. "And yet in a comparatively small space of time you have come to know each member of this family very well, *señorita.*"

"The—circumstances were—unusual, *señor*."

"Unusual? Yes, I agree. But nevertheless, you have to admit that your presence here in the valley has already caused no small upheaval."

Miranda sighed. "So we are going to talk about Juan and Lucy, *señor*."

Father Domenico uttered an ejaculation. "Only indirectly, *señorita*. I am not questioning Juan's fondness for you—for both of you. Doña Isabella is of the old school which clings to the—how do you say?—*matrimonio de convenieccia?*—the arranged marriage, *si?* She finds it hard to accept the fact that Juan has a mind of his own and refuses to be dominated any longer. Naturally, she was shocked. Naturally, she did not accept it at first. But gradually—"

"What are you trying to say, *señor*?" Miranda's stomach muscles were taut.

Father Domenico shrugged. "I am merely conveying that so far as Doña Isabella is concerned, there will be no further opposition to your—friendship—with Juan."

Miranda gasped. "Juan and I are not friends, *señor*. We are acquaintances. His—his behaviour over Lucy has destroyed any friendship there might have been between us!"

"But you do not understand what I am saying, *señorita*. You may stay in the valley with Doña Isabella's blessing. Both of you. Your problems are over."

Miranda thought they were only just beginning. "*Señor*—"

"*Momento, señorita*. We will discuss the matter of Juan and Lucy later." He held up his hand as she would have interrupted him, and said: "Please—let me finish what I have to say concerning Rafael." He waited until the animosity died out of her face and then went on: "The situation is this—since returning to the valley for his uncle's funeral, Rafael has become more and more involved with our life here. A priest does not do this. He

169

must always maintain a measure of—shall we say—detachment? Like a doctor, emotion must not enter into his ministry, do you understand? Rafael is not like this. He has allowed emotion to rule his head, I have seen it. And how could it be otherwise? He is the son of his father, no matter how he may rebel against his heritage."

"But why are you telling me all this?" exclaimed Miranda, still not fully understanding the implications so far as she was concerned. She was too bemused by it all, too confused.

Father Domenico finished his chocolate and made a gesture of appreciation. "Doña Isabella understands her sons' dilemmas, *señorita*. With my help she has come to appreciate the difficulties. As *patron*, Juan could not be permitted to marry a—stranger, *verdad*? But, if this is what he wants, and he is prepared to give up the estate . . ."

And suddenly, sickeningly, Miranda was aware of what all this had been leading up to. Whether or not Rafael had a vocation was not the question. Doña Isabella's sole concern was to bring her eldest son back into his rightful position. Hadn't she demonstrated time and again her preference for Rafael, her frustration that he found so little time to spend with her? He was her first-born, her favourite, that was obvious. And now, with the priest's help, she had devised this sanctioning of Juan's infatuation for the English girls in the hope that Rafael might feel obliged to step into his brother's shoes should Juan vacate them. And she never, for one moment, imagined that Rafael himself might be attracted to Miranda . . .

With a determined effort, Miranda got to her feet. "I'm afraid you've been wasting your time, *señor*. I cannot speak for—for Juan, of course, but so far as I am concerned any emotional relationship between us is purely imaginary. I don't love Juan! I don't even like him very much. And I'm pretty sure he doesn't love me!"

As Father Domenico stood up and faced her, a frown drawing his black brows together, there was a squeal of brakes from outside. Miranda recognised the sound of the Landrover and her stomach muscles tautened as footsteps came down the hall.

Rafael appeared in the doorway, but there was another man close behind him, a man Miranda thought she recognised and then told herself she was having hallucinations. Rafael looked tired and drawn, and her heart went out to him, but her eyes merely registered the presence of the priest before he stood stiffly aside. The other man entered the room and Miranda caught her breath. He was a tall man, who had once been heavily built but whose flesh now hung slackly, and he walked more heavily on one foot than the other.

"I believe you know this man, *señorita,* said Rafael abruptly, and Miranda moved her head slowly up and down.

Much thinner than she remembered, his shoulders slightly hunched beneath the ill-fitting grey suit, nevertheless Miranda would have known her brother-in-law anywhere. "Bob?" she whispered disbelievingly.

"Miranda," he said nodding, and then more strongly: "Miranda!" and she covered the space between them to be enclosed in his bearlike embrace.

CHAPTER ELEVEN

ON the journey up to the monastery to meet his daughter Bob Carmichael endeavoured to tell Miranda what had happened to him. But first he had told her that Susan was dead, and the faint hopes which had arisen inside her were doused for ever. And at least one of Lucy's parents was alive.

Squashed in the front of the Landrover between Bob and Rafael, Miranda tried to concentrate on what her brother-in-law was saying when all the while she was conscious of Rafael's thigh pressing against her own, and his shoulder slightly overlapping hers. Once she shifted a little and accidentally put a hand on his leg to support herself as she did so, only to attempt to withdraw it swiftly when she realised what she had done. But Rafael's right hand captured hers and secured it.

"There was one hell of a storm," Bob was saying. "The plane wasn't full and we were sitting near the back. I guess everyone forward of us was killed outright. We were losing altitude and those peaks seemed hellish close. I don't honestly know what happened. Maybe the tail tipped the rock-face, but whatever it was, it snapped off and the rest of the plane crashed down into this ravine." He shook his head. "I didn't know all this at the time, of course. Both Susan and I were badly injured. Oh, yes, Susan was still alive after the crash, but we both thought Lucy was dead. I think that was what destroyed Susan's will to hang on." He broke off, obviously emotionally disturbed, and Miranda felt a little of the depth of his grief.

"Anyway," he continued, at last, "Lucy must have been flung some distance away from the broken fusel-

172

age, because her body wasn't found. I assumed later that it had gone down the ravine." He sighed. "But I mustn't get ahead of myself, must I?" He shook his head. "Susan and I were the only survivors in the tail end of the fuselage."

"You were conscious!" Miranda broke out.

"Oh, yes. To begin with, at least. I don't remember a lot about what happened, but I do recall being almost frozen to death, and Susan's blood clotting on her head—" He broke off. "I'm sorry. I'm sorry! I don't mean to be morbid." He paused. "We were found, almost dead, I think, by some Indians from a remote mountain village. They didn't speak any English, of course, and by the time I was able to say anything Susan was already dead. I don't know how long I lay in that hut, hovering on the borderline between life and death—three, maybe four months, I don't know. The villagers were simple people. They had no medical supplies, no real contact with the outside world! Winter was pretty rough. I think if I'd died, no one would ever have heard of me again."

He looked across at Rafael. "Maybe you can understand this. Maybe you know these people. They're intensely independent. They used what skills they had to help me. If I was to die, they had done what they could."

Rafael's face was grave. "I am not an Indian, *señor*," he said quietly. "But they are honourable people."

Bob made an impatient gesture. "I'm not criticising what they did for me, *señor*. Nevertheless, no message was sent to the authorities that I was still alive, and not until I was able to walk and express my concern did word filter through that there was a foreign man living in this village in the mountains."

Rafael's mouth twisted ironically. "I very much doubt that these people had any contact with—what was it you said?—the authorities?" He shook his head. "*Autoridad* means something different to them, *señor*."

173

Bob was not convinced. "Well, anyway, eventually I made it down to a place called Suestra. I—I'm partially paralysed in this right leg, you see, and walking is not easy for me. But I was alive! I suppose that was about six weeks ago. It's taken me that long to identify myself, get some money and fly back to England. It wasn't until I went in search of her that David Hallam, Miranda's boss, gave me the news that my daughter might still be alive, too."

Miranda cast an awkward glance at Rafael's set face and then looked encouragingly at Bob. "You know that—that Lucy doesn't remember—anything, don't you?" she asked, reluctantly withdrawing her hand from Rafael's. There was something clandestine about their intense awareness of one another and while she wanted desperately to turn to Rafael she could not allow herself to do so. That way lay disaster and disillusion . . . Besides, Bob needed her. Rafael didn't.

Bob was nodding now. "I know. Don Rafael explained the position to me. I had just arrived at the hacienda and was talking to—er—Doña Isabella? Is that right? Yes? Well, I was talking with her when Don Rafael appeared. Apparently, she was telling me, her other son, Juan, has been quite taken with Lucy."

Miranda chanced another glance at Rafael, but he had transferred both his hands to the wheel now and seemed intent on negotiating the uneven terrain that led up to the white-walled monastery.

"Is that it?" exclaimed Bob, leaning forward and pointing.

"Yes," Miranda nodded. "Not very far now."

Bob uttered an eager cry and impulsively put one arm around her. "Oh Miranda! he muttered, pressing his face against her neck. "You've no idea what this means to me after all these months! Thank God I've got you now that Susan's gone. You'll help me with Lucy, won't you? Who knows—" He lifted his head and looked into her eyes. "Who knows, we might be able to make some-thing out, hmm?"

Miranda was horrified. "Oh, Bob, please," she be-gan, feeling the hot colour running up her neck to her face. "I—I—" she looked helplessly at Rafael and now encountered the full force of cold dark eyes before he turned his head sharply back to the road again.

Lucy came running out to greet them as usual. She had recognised the Landrover and perhaps she was hoping that Rafael was going to take her out again. Rafael swung down from the vehicle first, and a shy smile lifted the corners of the little girl's mouth. Then he reached into the Landrover and taking Miranda's wrist in a grip of steel drew her out, too.

"Miranda!" Lucy exclaimed excitedly, and the older girl was warmed by the enthusiasm in her voice which had seldom lifted in quite that way for her.

"Hello, love," she said, as Lucy came running to-wards her. "It's so good to see you again." And a lump formed in her throat as the little girl reached up to hug her.

"It's good to see you, too," she declared. "Tio Juan said you were ill and couldn't have visitors, but I wanted to see you. Tio Juan said we would go and see you together—maybe today!"

Miranda glanced over her shoulder at the Landrover. "Well, I'm here now, Lucy," she said encouragingly. "And—and I've brought someone else for you to meet."

Lucy took an automatic step backward. "Oh, yes?"

"Yes." Miranda caught her hand. "Darling, don't run away, please! Go—go and see who's in the Landrover. It—it's someone who's simply dying to see you. Some-one you love—very much."

Lucy hung back for a few more seconds and then on reluctant feet she took a few steps forward. She peered into the shadowy interior of the Landrover and then her eyes widened into enormous orbs of disbelief.

175

"It—it's—oh, no, it can't be, *it can't be*!" and she burst into hysterical sobs and would have rushed away had not Rafael caught her and propelled her determinedly back to the vehicle where Bob Carmichael was slowly getting out.

"Hello, Lucy," he said, as Rafael continued to hold her struggling little body between his hands. "You remember me, don't you? Say you remember me! Daddy's come such a long way to find you."

About three-quarters of an hour later, Rafael came to find Miranda.

She had been sitting on a broken stone wall that had once housed the supplies for the monastery, shadowed by the drunken beams that were all that was left of the roof of the building. She had been sitting there for quite some time after refusing Father Esteban's offer of refreshment. Bob and Lucy and Rafael had all gone into the building with the priest, but she had pleaded a need for air and been left alone.

She was trying to burgeon her spirits by reiterating the fact that now her father was here and Lucy was beginning the long haul back to full consciousness of her identity Juan no longer had any hold on her—on either of them.

But it didn't seem to work. Whether her days in bed had weakened her or whether it was simply the knowledge that there was nothing now to keep her in the valley, she didn't know, but she felt utterly depressed. So much for Father Domenico's machinations, she thought without malice. There was no longer any reason for Doña Isabella to hope that Juan might abandon his position on the estate and leave a gap that only Rafael could fill. No doubt she would not give up, maybe she would find some other method to keep her eldest son close to her, but Miranda would have no part of it.

She was not aware of Rafael's approach until he climbed the wall and came to stand in front of her. He was wearing tight-fitting denim pants that clung to his thighs and she would not lift her eyes above hip-level.

"I am about to take your brother-in-law and Lucy to the hacienda, *señorita*," he stated formally. "Señor Carmichael wishes to thank my mother and my brother for their hospitality. Are you ready to leave?"

Miranda twisted her hands together. "When—when does Bob expect to leave?"

"This afternoon." Rafael shrugged. "He came by automobile, but it is a long and uncomfortable journey by road. I have offered to take him to Puebla in the helicopter. His car and its *chofer* will leave this morning and meet him there."

"I see." Miranda swallowed convulsively. "Well, my things are at your house. I'll wait there until Bob has been to the hacienda and come back again—if—if you don't mind."

Rafael shifted his weight from one foot to the other. "You are leaving with your brother-in-law?" he asked harshly.

Miranda had to look up then. "Of course. Bob—Bob will need me. He—he's not much good around the house."

Rafael's expression darkened angrily. "You will *live* with him?"

Miranda made a helpless gesture. "Of course. Why not?"

Rafael shook his head. "When you are ready, *señorita* . . ."

Miranda got up, looking up at him anxiously. "What did you expect me to say, Rafael? I shan't be *sleeping* with him, if that's what you think."

Rafael turned away and climbed back over the wall. "The others are waiting, *señorita*," he said, and walked away.

London was damp and cold, and although it was July, it was nothing like summer.

Bob and Lucy had no home of their own, the Carmichaels having sold their house and stored the furniture when they first left for South America, so they moved in with Miranda for the time being. Not that Miranda minded. Since leaving Rafael in the reception lounge of the airport building at Puebla, she had felt drained of all emotion, and was glad of their presence to fill the empty flat.

Bob had no desire to resume working in South America, although the firm he worked for had offered him his old job back again. Instead, they agreed to him being seconded into the London office for a year to enable him to find his feet again.

Lucy started school the day Miranda returned to the bank, and that was when the problems began.

Not that individually they had problems. Bob was clearly glad to be in harness again; David Hallam was so relieved that Miranda had come back to take over from a rather inferior stand-in that he forgot to be angry that the two weeks' absence had lengthened into four; and Lucy found school quite a novelty after being free for so long.

But school finished at four o'clock, and Miranda was first home at around five-thirty, which meant that Lucy would be alone for fully an hour and a half.

To begin with, Miranda managed to arrange with David to work her lunch hour and leave at four o'clock too. David didn't like it, but afraid of losing her again, he agreed to a limited period. However, at the end of two weeks when Bob had made no effort to make other arrangements, Miranda broached the subject.

"I've been thinking about it," he replied, in answer to her queries. "What I really need is a housekeeper, isn't it? But we don't have room for a housekeeper here."

Keeping her own feelings out of it, Miranda said:

"You could move—get another flat, or a house. You could employ a housekeeper, Bob. You can afford one."

"I know that." Bob moved closer to her on the couch. Lucy was in bed. She shared Miranda's room while Bob slept on this bed settee. "Miranda, I don't want to employ a housekeeper. I want you to marry me—No! Wait!" as she would have interrupted him. "I know it's too soon. I know Susan hasn't been dead a year yet, but can't you see that would be the ideal solution?"

Miranda sprang up from the couch. "No, Bob," she said, definitely. "No. That's impossible."

"Why? Why is it impossible? There's no one else. No one serious, that is. You've told me that your feelings for Hallam don't match his for you. Why is it such an impossibility?"

"Because I don't love you, Bob." Miranda spread her hands. "Please—you've got to believe me. I shan't change my mind."

Bob hunched his shoulders. He had a defeated look and she felt sorry for him, but that wasn't sufficient basis for a marriage.

"You realise if you turn me down I shall look for someone else, don't you?" he asked quietly. "It's no good, Miranda. I'm not a man who can live alone. Susan knew this. She would understand. Are you sure you're not letting your feelings for her blind you to the suitability of this situation?"

"No. No, of course not." Miranda shook her head vigorously. "Please—do as you like. Look for a house, or a flat. Employ someone for Lucy. I'll come and see you as often as I can, but I can't marry you, Bob."

After that, the situation between them was somewhat strained. Miranda had not realised how subtly he had insinuated himself into her life, sharing the cooking with her, drying dishes, generally making himself useful. Once he knew Miranda had no intention of marrying

179

him, he took to leaving his things about in an untidy fashion, never drying dishes, never entering the kitchen unless it was to ask her something and she happened to be there. Fortunately, Lucy seemed not to notice the change and for her sake Miranda tried to behave as if nothing was wrong.

But at last Bob announced that he had found an apartment. He was arranging for the furniture that was in store to be delivered the next day and he and Lucy would be leaving in two days. Miranda tried to show enthusiasm, but Bob's attitude left little room for friendship. She had never felt so alone, not even in the valley. Always then, she had had Lucy to think of—now she had no one.

The worst time was coming home on the evening after Bob and Lucy had moved—to an empty flat. David had invited her out to dinner that evening, sensing that she would feel lonely without any company, and she had gratefully accepted. He was calling for her at seven-thirty, and she ran up the steps at five-thirty she reflected that she had only two hours to get through before his arrival. Only two hours . . . It could seem a lifetime.

She inserted her key in the lock and opened the door into the lounge. Then she halted aghast at the sight of a man stretched out on the bed settee. She thought for a minute that Bob had come back, that something had happened to Lucy, but her entrance had disturbed her visitor and as he got slowly to his feet her handbag dropped from her nerveless fingers and she fell back against the closing door so that it slammed behind her.

"*Rafael!*" she breathed weakly. "Oh, God, it is you, isn't it? I—I'm not dreaming this, am I?"

He moved towards her, grasping her wrists and drawing her towards him, wrapping her arms around his back, forcing her so closely against him that she was left in no doubt that this was the substance, not the shadow. For a moment he just held her closely against him, and

180

then he drew back and looked down into her face.

"Dream—or nightmare?" he demanded huskily, and she felt her lips trembling as she stammered: "Dream—oh, yes, dream, Rafael!"

And then he was kissing her, over and over again, hungry urgent kisses that left her in no doubt of his need for her. He muttered to her in his own language, between kisses, against her throat and her neck and her mouth, his hands tangled in her hair, caressing her, intimately taking possession of her in a way that hitherto she had not experienced. "Mine," he muttered, with intense satisfaction. "Mine, are you not?"

Miranda didn't answer him. It was enough to be in his arms. She didn't want to question the rights and wrongs of something that might so easily evaporate in the cooler temperature of common sense.

But at last Rafael held her away from him, looking with undisguised pleasure at her dishevelled appearance—her tangled hair, her bare mouth and flushed cheeks, the rounded swell of her breasts visible between the buttons he had unfastened on her shirt.

"Hmm," he murmured, his mouth frankly sensuous. "You are a witch, Miranda. You have cast a spell on me. Without you, I am an empty vessel."

Miranda twisted in his hands, half embarrassed at his intent appraisal, but he would not let her go. "Do not be ashamed, *querida*," he said huskily. "You have a beautiful body—and I intend to possess every centimetre of it, do you understand?" Then his hands dropped to his sides. "Do you not want to know why I am here?"

Miranda's fingers fumbled for the buttons on her shirt, but his hands stayed hers. "See," he groaned, pulling her against him again, "I cannot keep my hands from you. *Dios* come closer to me—closer. Oh, Miranda, I do so badly want to love you!"

Miranda's senses were inflamed. His words were more intoxicating than wine. But she tore herself away from him, putting the settee between them. "Why—why are you here, Rafael?" she asked, forcing a calmness she was far from feeling.

If she had expected him to be angry at her withdrawal she was pleasantly surprised. Instead, he took up a position before the empty hearth and said: "I am here because I am in love with you, Miranda. I think I have been in love with you for quite a long time."

Miranda pressed her hands together. "But—but —your career—"

"What career?" His eyes caressed her. "I have several."

Miranda gripped the back of the settee. "Don't tease me, Rafael. Constancia told me you were—you were to enter the priesthood."

Rafael's expression became grave. "Yes. Yes, I was."

"Then how can you give it up so lightly—"

"I do not give it up lightly," he corrected her, his voice hardening a fraction. "But since meeting you I have realised that I do not have the vocation I once imagined I possessed—"

"But you didn't—" Miranda shifted restlessly. "Rafael, never at any time did you lead me to believe—" She broke off biting her lips. "Has—has Father Domenico persuaded you to change your mind?"

"Father Domenico?" Rafael frowned. "Why should Father Domenico persuade me to change my mind?"

Miranda shook her head, her lips pressed tightly together. Then she burst out: "Your mother wanted you to give it up, didn't she? She thought if—if I were to marry Juan and he had to leave the estate you would be forced to take it over! But then Bob came and—well, the situation changed, didn't it? I wondered if they'd try something else, and they have—they have!" Her voice broke on a sob, and in a moment Rafael was beside her, drawing her resisting body into his arms.

"What are you talking about?" he murmured gently,

pressing her face into his chest. She had unfastened his shirt earlier and as he had made no move to button it again her cheek was against the hair-roughened skin. "Do you honestly suppose, knowing my mother as you do, that she would encourage me to leave the priesthood to marry, not only an English girl, but a Protestant into the bargain? Oh, no, *querida,* you were not her choice."

Miranda couldn't take it all in. Had he actually said he intended marrying her?

"But you didn't explain . . ." she whispered.

"What is there to explain?" Rafael spoke urgently, as though for not much longer he would continue to control his emotions. "All right, all right. If it is explanations you want, I will give them to you. I was—attracted to you from the beginning. I think you were aware of this, too, were you not? It was my first experience of a doubt which was to fill my days with indecision, my nights with despair. I had set myself above such things, and I was finding myself as sick with longing for you as any unrequited suitor."

"Oh, Rafael!"

"*Si.* I was so jealous of Juan, of the twins, of anyone who came into contact with you, and yet I myself kept away, unable to guarantee my own behaviour. That day at the lake, when I lay with you on the beach, I think I would have made love to you then had I not been so acutely aware of the child. You knew I wanted you, didn't you?" And at her half-embarrassed nod, he smiled wryly: "No wonder I was so shaken on the journey back. You thought I was ill. I was—but not from any physical malady." He shook his head reminiscently. "And finally, there was the night at my house when I so nearly took that irrevocable step. Why did you stop me? Did you not realise that once I had lain with you I would never have left you? I am not like these other men you have known. This time it will be for life, *amada,* make no mistake."

183

Miranda drew herself unsteadily out of his arms. "I—I don't understand, Rafael. Do—do you think my refusal that night at—at your house was through fear? Fear that you might leave me? What do you mean—you are not like other men I have known?"

Rafael tried to draw her back into his arms, but she resisted him. "What does it matter what I think?" he demanded impatiently. "I am here now—we are together—" He sighed. "I have not always been honourable, Miranda. Once, when I was younger, when my father was alive—there were many women. I thought I was sick of women—and then I met you."

She tore herself away from him and walked to the door. "I'd like you to leave now, please," she said unevenly.

Rafael stared at her incredulously. "Miranda—"

"No, I mean it. Your mother will never accept me as your—woman."

"My wife," he corrected gravely, crossing the room to stand by the door she had opened. "My mother is most eager to welcome you to the hacienda. After you left three weeks ago, I could no longer fool myself that it was possible to put you out of my mind. You were in my thoughts every minute of the day. I had to see you again, to find out whether you might conceivably feel the same. I told my mother I intended to marry you, if you would have me. Can you imagine the furore that caused? And then, when she was calmer, she said that if I would return to the hacienda, she would approve our marriage. I would have married you anyway, you understand? But if I had her approval, so much the better. However, that was not all I wanted. I have her agreement to divide the lands of the estate between the tenants. Everyone shall work for themselves in future, and not for the aggrandisement of an inanimate hunk of land, *verdad?*" He turned to go out of the door. "I am sorry you do not feel as I do. My apologies."

The door closed behind him, leaving Miranda more shattered than before. Had he meant everything he had said? Had he really come here with the intention of marrying her?

She wrenched open the door, his name on her lips, but the passage was empty, there were no steps on the stair. He had gone!

She closed the door again and sought the settee. Then with trembling fingers she reached for the phone. She could not go out with David Hallam this evening. She doubted she would ever go out with any man ever again.

By midnight, she had rung all the major hotels she could think of where she thought he might be staying and drawn a blank. She lay in her bed, sleepless and dry-eyed, unable to believe that she had been stupid enough to send him away. Was she such a prude? Was she so proud? Rafael had had every reason to suppose she had had lovers. His was not a society like hers where women could live as the equals of men without giving more of themselves than they wished. He could only have seen her behaviour as reckless, and yet—in spite of everything—he still wanted to marry her! Or he had. Who knew what he might feel now?

She pressed her face into the pillow, wishing she could cry. Anything to destroy this façade of numbness that made her head and stomach ache with suppressed emotion.

And then she heard the sound of a key being inserted in the lock of the outer door and she jack-knifed upright, her whole body tensing. Rafael still had a key, she thought dazedly. Had he come back? Or had he returned the key to Bob and he had thought to come and try and persuade her to change her mind? The idea that it might be an intruder did not occur to her.

She slid out of bed, pulling on her robe. It was an unusually warm night and since returning from Mexico she had taken to sleeping without clothes. She opened her bedroom door a crack and peered through. There were no lights yet, but a shadowy figure was silently closing the outer door. Her heart rose suffocatingly into her throat and almost choked her.

"Rafael?" she whispered desperately, "is that you, Rafael?"

He touched the switch and lamplight flooded the room "Who were you expecting, *querida*?" he enquired mockingly, dropping a parcel on to the couch, and with a little cry she sped across the room and into his arms.

Between kisses, she murmured incoherently: "But why—why did you go? Why did you leave me to worry myself sick about you?"

"And is not that what I have been doing since the moment I first laid eyes on you?" he demanded huskily. "I gather you wanted me to come back, after all."

"Oh, yes, yes!" She pressed herself closely against him, feeling his immediate response. "Oh, Rafael, I love you!" And she wound her arms around his neck and kissed him.

For several minutes there was silence in the flat, and then Rafael roused himself, his eyes glazed with emotion. "And you will marry me?" he commanded, and she nodded eagerly.

"As soon as you like." She paused. "Why did you go away? Just to teach me a lesson?"

Rafael half smiled. "Partly. And partly to bring you this parcel. I think you forget I still have your pants and shirt, *no*?"

Miranda gasped, "I'd forgotten!"

"I had not." Rafael's mouth twisted with self-derision. "I have kept them close to me ever since they came into my possession."

"Oh, Rafael!" She shook her head. "But where have you been to take so long? Where are you staying?"

"I have a distant cousin who is a priest working at a

hospital run by the fathers at a place called Maidenhead, do you know it?" And at her nod, he went on: "My cousin invited me to stay with him and I agreed. I did not expect to get to you so easily. I had thought—but no matter."

"No. What had you thought?" Miranda wanted to know.

"Well, I admit, I had thought your brother-in-law would be here. I expected to have to—persuade you to leave him."

"Rafael!" She stared at him indignantly.

"Well—" He moved his shoulders apologetically. "No matter—you were here, and you were—beautiful! I did not want to leave you, but perhaps I thought it was best—then." He sighed. "I drive back to my cousin's apartments and then I find I cannot relax. I tell myself I will come back tomorrow, but it is no good. I have to know—tonight."

Miranda pressed her hot cheeks against his chest. "And now?"

Rafael shrugged. "That is up to you. We will fly back to Mexico as soon as possible. We will get married there—in the chapel. Father Domenico would wish to perform the service, you understand? Naturally your brother-in-law and Lucy are welcome to join us for the celebrations. I will arrange the matter of tickets, of course."

"Oh, Rafael!" Miranda looked up at him adoringly. "You don't know how happy you've made me."

Rafael gathered her closer against him. "And you, *querida*? Now will you make me happy?" he demanded possessively.

"If that's what you want." Miranda could not deny him.

But Rafael only held her for a few moments before pushing her away from him. "No," he said huskily, shaking his head. "No, we will wait. I am not worthy of you, *amada*." He smiled. "Go to bed, *querida*," he insisted, his eyes caressing. "Go to bed before I change my mind for purely selfish reasons!"

Four weeks later, Miranda and Rafael were married in the little chapel in the valley. All the villagers were there, as well as the Cueras family and their relations. Miranda wore a white lace dress that had once belonged to Rafael's mother, and she was given away by Bob, with Lucy as bridesmaid. Even Juan seemed totally quiescent to his new position as estate mananger, and he was having another house built some distance from the hacienda for himself, his mother, and his sisters. Valentina was back in the picture, and somehow Miranda sensed it would not be long before she and her mother succeeded in persuading him that the betrothal should be renewed.

For herself, Rafael was all she needed. She didn't care where they lived, in the magnificent hacienda, or in the stone house down by the river. So long as they were together, nothing else mattered.

On the morning following their wedding night, she awoke in the villa at Acapulco, which he had taken for their honeymoon, to find Rafael lying watching her, a lazy smile lifting the corners of his mouth.

She stretched sensuously, aware of his gaze and revelling in it, and said "Well? Was I satisfactory?"

Rafael laughed, and buried his face between her breasts. "Oh, Miranda," he muttered, desire banishing his amusement, "I'm sorry if I hurt you."

Her fingers tangled themselves in his hair and she drew his head up to hers. "Only at first," she admitted huskily. "And afterwards—oh, Rafael, you do believe me now, don't you?"

Rafael looked down at her caressingly. "My woman," he said wonderingly. "Yes, I believe you, Miranda. And dare I admit that I'm old-fashioned enough to be glad you never belonged to anyone else but me."

Mills & Boon
Best Seller Romances

The very best of Mills & Boon Romances
brought back for those of you who missed
them when they were first published.

In July
we bring back the following four
great romantic titles.

FIRE AND ICE
by Janet Dailey

To fulfil the terms of her mother's will Alisa had to be
married before she was allowed to look after her young half-
sister, and Zachary Stuart was the only man prepared to
marry her. But Alisa's idea of marriage differed very much
from that of her new husband!

THE IMPOSSIBLE MARRIAGE
by Lilian Peake

Old Mrs. Dunlopp thought it was a splendid idea to leave her
large house and a lot of money to her great-nephew Grant Gard
and her young friend Beverley Redmund — on condition that
within six months they got married. There was one snag: the
two people concerned just couldn't stand each other!

WIND RIVER
by Margaret Way

Perri had come here to Coorain, in the Dead Heart of Australia,
to work, not to teeter on the brink of disaster with a man like
the cattle baron Gray Faulkner. But how could she avoid it?

THE GIRL AT GOLDENHAWK
by Violet Winspear

Jaine was used to taking back place to her glamorous cousin
Laraine, and as it seemed only natural to Laraine and her
mother that Jaine should take on the difficult task of explaining
to her cousin's wealthy suitor that she had changed her mind
about the marriage, Jaine nerved herself to meet the arrogant
Duque Pedro de Ros Zanto. But there was a surprise in store . . .

If you have difficulty in obtaining any of these books through
your local paperback retailer, write to:

Mills & Boon Reader Service
P.O. Box 236, Thornton Road, Croydon, Surrey CR9 3RU.

Take romance with you on your holiday.

Holiday time is almost here again. So look out for the special Mills & Boon Holiday Reading Pack.* Four new romances by four favourite authors. Attractive, smart, easy to pack and only £3.00.

*Available from 12th June.

Dakota Dreamin'
Janet Dailey

Devil Lover
Carole Mortimer

Forbidden Flame
Anne Mather

Gold to Remember
Mary Wibberley

Mills & Boon
The rose of romance

Mills & Boon
Best Seller Romances

The very best of Mills & Boon
brought back for those of you
who missed reading them when they
were first published.
There are three other Best Seller Romances
for you to collect this month.

COVE OF PROMISES
by Margaret Rome

With her schooldays in Paris behind her Elise could hardly wait
for her return to Jamaica to be reunited with Jacques, from
whom she had been parted for ten years. Jacques, her childhood
sweetheart, to whom she would soon be married. But Elise was
to find reality very different from the dreams she had cherished,
and the man she thought she knew now seemed an aloof
stranger . . .

COUNTRY OF THE VINE
by Mary Wibberley

Although Charlotte had led a sheltered life she was sure she
could cope with anything that could be considered a problem.
Until, in a French vineyard, she met Jared, the man whose dark
attraction she had never forgotten.

THE VIKING STRANGER
by Violet Winspear

What a fascinating man Erik Norlund was, Jill thought. She
couldn't be sure which facet of him came uppermost — the
smooth American tycoon, or the more rugged characteristics
of his Viking forebears. She got her chance to find out when
Erik offered her a job in his luxury department store in sunny
California.

If you have difficulty in obtaining any of these books through
your local paperback retailer, write to:

Mills & Boon Reader Service
P.O. Box 236, Thornton Road, Croydon, Surrey, CR9 3RU.